# TANYA TANIA

Born in Kolkata, Antara Ganguli grew up in Bombay. Her interest in India-Pakistan started with the 1992 riots when she wrote down the names of the girls in her class to identify who was Hindu and who was Muslim.

Antara has written for *The Atlantic Monthly, The Wall Street Journal, Stanford Social Innovation Review, Times of India, Indian Express* and others. She is a 2014 Asia Society Young Leaders Fellow and a 2015 Sangam House Fellow. She works in international development and currently lives in Dhaka, Bangladesh.

# TANYA TANIA

A novel by
**Antara Ganguli**

# BLOOMSBURY
NEW DELHI • LONDON • OXFORD • NEW YORK • SYDNEY

First published in India 2016

© 2016 by Antara Ganguli

ISBN 978 93 84898 41 0
2 4 6 8 10 9 7 5 3 1

Bloomsbury Publishing India Pvt. Ltd
Second Floor, LSC Building No.4
DDA Complex, Pocket C – 6 & 7, Vasant Kunj
New Delhi 110070
www.bloomsbury.com

Typeset by Manmohan Kumar
Printed and bound in India by Gopsons Papers Ltd

To find out more about our authors and books visit www.bloomsbury.com.
Here you will find extracts, author interviews, details of forthcoming
events and the option to sign up for our newsletters.

*for my father*
*Ram Shankar Ganguli*

# 1

February 4, 1996
New York, NY

Dear Tania,

Last night there was a snowstorm that made my window disappear. I woke up thinking you had died. This is my first letter in three and a half years. First letter since I left Pakistan. First letter since Nusrat.

I am going to keep writing to you. If you never reply, you'll still get my letters, slipping under your door like you had said, in the middle of somnolent afternoons, right before the perfect time for tea. You will not be home. You will be at college. And then one day, you will be in an office somewhere. And then who knows where, perhaps not even in India, but my letters will keep slipping under the door. Until you forgive me. And after then.

Uncurl your lip, dearest. I am not assuming you will forgive me. I don't even think you should forgive me. But I will keep writing to you. I have to write to you. I have to keep writing to you.

It is the deep dark centre of winter here in New York. The worst part, really. Days go dark by five and my grandfather died over winter break. I have trouble eating and lost eleven pounds somewhere in the snowdrifts. It is my last semester and truth: I love seeing my ribs in the mirror. My body beautiful.

*It is impossible that I used to think summer in Karachi was unbearable but I did according to my letters to you. I crave the sun now, I crave sweat. I go to the gym and run and crank and pull and push just to feel it form over my shoulders and down my back. I push my tongue into the crevice of my upper lip and lick the drop there. Secretly, always secretly because otherwise people will think you're crazy.*

*Everyone has so many secrets. I never knew that before. Afterwards, I saw secrets everywhere. Streaming out of noses, rising above heads, disgorged and smeared on lips like a drunk girl's lipstick.*

*Here's a secret! You were right, Ali IS gay! He came out to me when I was in the hospital for mad people. We are all weird, he told me.*

*How prescient of you, T. How very clever. Here's another secret. What I really want to say:*

*Dear Tania,*

*You were right. I was wrong. Now please forgive me because I'm hoping that will make it stop.*

*Love,*
*Tanya*

*What do you think? It doesn't matter. I will still write to you. This is only a first letter.*

~

Feb 14, 1991
*Karachi*

Dear Tania,
    Hello. My name is Tanya Talati and I am the daughter of Lisa Talati, your mother's friend. They were at Wellesley College together. In college, my mother was Lisa Wilking. You must have heard of us.

It is at my mother's suggestion that I am writing to you. I broke my leg playing hockey and have to remain in bed with an immobilized knee. It is stultifying. I am reading my way through the American classics so that I will be well prepared for writing college admission essays. I'm reading Hemingway right now. He is alright. Not quite as dark as Dostoyevsky, who is my favourite.

I thought perhaps you'd be interested in exchanging letters with me. Not in the manner of pen-pals as we are not strangers. We have a picture of you and your brother in our living room. You are a baby in a yellow dress sitting on your mother's lap and your brother's hands are around your throat. Congratulations on his admission to Princeton.

Which American colleges are you going to apply to? I am going to apply to twelve colleges, including three backup colleges. My top choice is Harvard. You don't have to tell me yours if you don't want to but I should tell you though, that everyone in school comes to me to help them pick colleges. They phone me in the evenings and ask me about their chances of getting in. Sometimes I get two or three phone calls in one night.

I have formulated a recuperation strategy for the three months it will take for me to be mobile again. Writing to you is on the list but its continued place and rank depends on you. Right now you're Number 2, right above Chhoti Bibi and right below getting a handle on the family finances.

I hope you will write back. My mother seems to think that we will become best friends. I have explained to her that this is unlikely but just so things are transparent between us, you should know that I left it a little vague. I don't like to upset her.

Anyway, it would be nice to hear from you. This broken knee means no hockey championship for me this year (and with Natasha at the helm, that means no hockey championship for anyone). No summer in Boston at my grandparents' with a shot at winning the Breaststroke 400 metres next year. No internship in a lawyer's office. My room has a sick person smell. Although Chhoti Bibi says it doesn't smell and she's the only other person who has been in it.

I hope you will write back. What's life in Bombay like? Is it anything like the movies?

Yours sincerely,
Tanya Talati

~

*March 2, 1991*
*Bombay*

Dear Tanya,

A movie about Bombay teenagers? BORING! I mean, not me. My life is really hectic. Between school and keeping my mom off my back and trying to keep my boyfriend from having sex with me (or anyone else), I really don't have time to write to you.

From your letter you sound like a Boring Person. But you play hockey. Do you play hockey in a salwar kameez? Because my mom said you wear a salwar kameez to school. That's cruel.

In my school, which is like the best school in Bombay, only boys play hockey. My brother says I should force them to change the rules. He says it's sexist. Now that he's left and gone to college in America, suddenly everything in India is shit.

Yeah, my mum talks about Lisa Aunty and you and your brother all the time. What's it like having an American mother? Does she like living in Pakistan?

What's it like having a twin brother? Sammy is two years older than me. He's cleverer than me but I have more friends. Like when I broke my leg, there used to be a line of people outside my bedroom. My dad put up a super cute sign saying VISITING

HOURS FOR THE STAR. My dad does really cute things like that. My mom gets mad at him for doing things like that. A lot of things make her mad.

Your brother is cute in the pictures your mom sends us at Christmas. Is he cute in real life?

By the way, you are OBSESSED with college. If I was even half as obsessed as you, my mom would love me. Actually she's the one making me write back to you but she told me not to tell you that. But I'm super honest.

I can't believe you actually want to go to Harvard and actually want to LIVE there for four years! I hate Harvard. My mother made me visit over the summer. It was like the World Conference of Boring People. I wanted to laugh about how everyone looked like a Boring Person but there was no one to laugh with because EVERYONE was a Boring Person. A BP. If you say BP really fast it sounds like a fart except it's an oil company.

Are you really good at hockey? I'm good at all sports. Like really good. I've won a shitload of awards. There is a whole shelf in the school prize cupboard right when you enter the principal's office that is just full of prizes that have my name on it except this one prize that is for Hindi debates. I keep waiting for them to throw it away but they haven't yet.

Being good at sports is super easy for me. Sammy has the brains gene, I have the sports gene. I'm also the most popular person in the family but that comes from no gene, you have to work super hard at it. And sometimes you have to be mean to people. I've been mean to so many people in my life, I don't even remember all of them. Like the other day I just picked up a book that had fallen from a girl's desk and she looked so surprised. I mean I can pick up a book you know. I'm not a monster.

I am though. Sometimes.

My parents fought about you today. Don't get excited, my parents fight about everything. And it's not like they fought about you exactly. Like I asked my mom about you at dinner and I asked about what your school uniform is and she said it's a salwar kameez and my dad was like I'm surprised they don't make them wear burkhas and then my mom called him racist and then they started arguing again and I got up and left because that's the best time to use the phone.

If my mother let me do laser treatment for my pimples I could relax a little because it's easier for hot people to be popular. I asked my dad if being hot matters as much when you're grown up and he said that when you're an adult, money replaces looks. Actually he said, 'Money replaces everything.' But he said it in that way where they're not really talking to you even though it sounds like they are.

So tell me more about this hockey stuff. Are you really the captain? Do you have a boyfriend?

Love,
Tania

P.S. Has your mother started the Wellesley Alumni Association in Pakistan? I'm pretty sure my mom started the Wellesley Alumni Association in India just so she can get me into Wellesley. I hate Wellesley almost as much as I hate Harvard.

~

*March 20, 1991*
*Karachi*

Dear Tania,

I wasn't going to respond to your rude letter but I admit, my curiosity is piqued. If your boyfriend is trying to have sex with other girls, why is he your boyfriend?

Let me take this opportunity to clarify some of your misconceptions.

One, it's really none of your business whether I have a boyfriend or not but just to set the record straight, I do. His name is Ali Naqvi. He is extremely good-looking. He is a painter and is very creative which is a good match for me because I am logical, rational and unemotional. I'm going to be a lawyer.

Ali Naqvi has never ever tried to have sex with me.

Two, having a twin brother is far worse than having a big brother. When your twin brother is Navi, it is like having no brother at all.

Three, no we do not play hockey in salwar kameezes. We play in shorts. I suppose now we are much cooler?

And finally, no, my mother did not start an alumni association. My mother is not one to start things.

Your letter demonstrates a sad lack of intellectual curiosity. I admit I am disappointed. Is it not at all interesting to you to consider a correspondence with your mother's best friend's daughter? We could find out from each other what our mothers were like in college. Do you have any pictures of them from that time? All the pictures in our house are from after we moved to Pakistan.

Chhoti Bibi is here so I must go. I've taught her to play chess with me. She's terrible but it's better than nothing.

                                                            Tanya

~

*March 30, 1991*
*Bombay*

Dear Tanya,
    Your boyfriend sounds gay. You better send me a picture.

My boyfriend is the best-looking boy in school. I'm saying that objectively. Even my mother thinks he's good looking and my mother hates him. There are a couple of boys in 12th who are better looking but they're boring good-looking you know? Like I can't deny Arjun has a weird nose. His eyes are scary because he's the intense, staring type. His hair stands up and he won't let me touch it because he spends hours punking it up.

He punks it up damn well.

It was quite hard to get him to fall for me. I have lots of experience in making guys fall for me. It usually takes two months, three if he's already with someone. But with Arjun, it took six months. Sometimes I think that he purposely made it that way so that I'd be stuck.

Sometimes I wish I hadn't done it.

When Arjun dresses up, he looks like a model. Every morning I wait to see him stride into class, always late, always hair half wet, always looking like the world is a joke and only he knows the punchline. He keeps our relationship a secret in school. I've thought about breaking up with him a thousand times. I'll tell him, look baby either we're together in front of everyone or we're not. But then when no one else is watching, he looks straight at me and I can't breathe.

What's Mr. Naqvi's story? Is he also reading the correct writers for college admissions? Do you do homework on your dates? Do you even have dates? Tell me the truth. Did you make him up?

So Nusrat said I should say sorry for my first letter. I mean I didn't think it was that bad but whatever. Sorry.

So who is this Chhoti Bibi chick? Your dad's first wife? Ha ha.

Love,
Tania

PS—Seriously man, I was just kidding about the first wife thing. Don't get your panties in a bunch.

~

*April 9, 1991*
*Karachi*

Dear Tania,

It is a testament to how bored I am that I continue to write to you. But my options are limited. I choose you.

Chhoti Bibi (thanks for the unnecessary translation) is the niece of Bibi. Bibi is our servant. She runs our house and all of us, including my mother, which is odd now that I think of it, because I remember when my mother used to run the house and Bibi.

Chhoti Bibi showed up at our house three months ago. She ran away from her village because she was married off to someone she didn't like. She bit him on their wedding night. Then she broke a window and escaped. It took a week to find her. By then the husband's family wouldn't have her back so they sent her to us. She's learning how to be a servant.

Chhoti Bibi comes and sits with me twice a day. I suspect she does it for the air conditioning. I don't really mind. There's something about her although I can't say what it is. She is a big girl who likes to wear green and yellow salwar kameezes with huge nylon flowers on them. Her hair is always oiled into fat, tight plaits with a fluorescent pink ribbon threading through them all the way up to a narrow river of scalp at the exact centre of her head. If Chhoti Bibi has ever heard of colours that don't give you a headache, she has shown no indication of it yet.

I suppose it's strange to discuss a servant quite so much. It's the broken knee. I don't see anyone these days other than Chhoti Bibi.

But still. There is something about her. Her first day here, she strode into the house and walked straight to the kitchen although there's no way she could have known where it was. She caused an uproar that morning by letting in a strange dog who relieved himself on the hall carpet that she then proceeded to wash with great enthusiasm, not realizing it was a fragile heirloom and Bibi almost had a heart attack when she saw it hanging on the line between our panties and pyjamas.

The other day, the gardener tried to be fresh with her and she slapped him. Right across the face. He lost his balance and fell into the pond and she went in and saved him which was quite unnecessary as the pond is only about three feet deep. The gardener was so insulted he tried to quit three times and had to be given the weekend off to drink and recover his self-esteem.

And was she embarrassed? No, not Chhoti Bibi. She came to my room and squatted in front of the AC, flinging her plaits over her shoulders so the air played over the nape of her neck and asked me to tell her the story of how my parents met. This has now become a daily ritual. Her conclusion to it is always, 'And then Baji was born, looking like a fairy doll.'

Baji of course is me. Fairy doll is courtesy my mother from whom I have inherited golden hair and pale eyes. Chhoti Bibi is obsessed with my hair. She spends hours combing it and building it into fanciful styles. It doesn't bother me. I'm resigned to how I look. Besides, it's nice when she plays with my hair. Nice to be touched. But I can't wait to go back to America where it was normal to be me.

Chhoti Bibi is my ticket to America, Tania. I've been wrestling for years with the problem of how to stand out in college applications and I think I have finally found it. You see, she dropped out of school in Class Eight. So she doesn't have a high school diploma. Don't you think if I managed to get her to pass the correspondence course equivalent of a high school degree, Harvard would find that impressive?

What do you think? Wouldn't you be impressed if you were an Admissions Officer at Harvard?

Best,
Tanya

~

*April 20, 1991*
*Bombay*

Dear Tanya,

You're damn boring. You're one giant college application. It's DAMN boring. Your letter sucked. Everything today sucked anyway but your letter sucked the hardest because it forced me to realize that even when I graduate from my stupid school which seems to attract Boring People like a magnet, I will still be surrounded by Boring People.

My mother is the world's biggest Boring Person. She fights with everyone. With me, with my dad, with the driver, with the cook.

I want to run away to an island somewhere near Goa and live there alone. Or maybe with Nusrat. Except I don't even want to mention Nusrat to you because of the way you talked about Chhoti Bibi which clearly shows that on top of being a Boring Person you have no class because you don't know how to talk to servants and my mom says that class is about how you talk to people especially poor people like servants.

Peace,
Tania

PS—Nusrat is not a servant.

# 2

*February 18, 1996*
*New York, NY*

*Dear Tania,*

*Today I went for a five-hour walk. You can do that in New York. Just finish your homework, put on your jacket and go outside and walk and walk and walk and walk. Train your gaze on the sidewalk, watch it come, watch it go. Soon you develop a rhythm, soon you start to feel warm, soon your footfall becomes a soundtrack, soon the crowds dissolve and the constant blur of faces is like the wind, a companion. Winter in New York is beautiful.*

*I needed to go for a walk because I was thinking about Jake. And you. I was luxuriating over this second letter. What will I say? What to pick from the last three and a half years and set out like ingredients for a meal I'm going to cook slowly and carefully for you? What not to say in case I offend you. I've decided to ask you nothing.*

*The most important thing to tell you is that my mother is much, much better. I wanted to write that she is a different person now but I can't in all honesty say that. She is still very thin and some days she doesn't leave the house. I wish she would take up a job instead of volunteering at the library. My grandfather left her everything when he died. And she was already living in their* house. I asked her if it feels good to not have to worry about having money anymore but she looked at me blankly. I don't think she notices having it any more than she had noticed not having it in Pakistan. Then what was it that made her leave my father and our life in Pakistan? She hasn't gone back once in three and a half years.

Guess what I'm majoring in! Well, I have two majors but this one is purely fun. No really, guess! You can't? Alright, I'll tell you.

My second major, my FUN major, is English Language and Literature. I bet you didn't see that coming, did you! My professor used to be Robert Frost's star pupil. He's grumpy and sarcastic and exacting and is the only professor who doesn't make me conscious of being depressed in snowflake land. He is also the only professor other than Amrita who wasn't surprised when I opened my mouth and a Pakistani accent came out. Professor Pritch asked me no questions other than if I thought Macaulay was racist. I told him I did.

This semester I have to take a class that I've been avoiding. It's integral to my serious major and really, I should have taken it before. Today Amrita made it clear to me in her supremely gentle yet iron way that I don't have a choice. Amrita is my thesis advisor. She's a professor of Political Science, specializing in Post-Colonial Studies. Amrita is brilliant and kind which is not common among professors. Amrita looks at me as if she knows everything. Paige says she has eyebrows of empathy.

Incidentally, it turns out Columbia is quite full of Boring People. You would have hated it. I wonder how you're liking Xavier's College. I have tried to imagine it. According to Mala, a lot of film stars go there. You should be a film star, Tania. You're gorgeous.

But anyway, I've made some friends. Two of them, Shahana and Mala, are Indian and I can't tell if you would love them or detest them. It drives me mad not being able to tell. Every friend I make, every boy I kiss, every party I go to, I want to know instantly what

you would think. Sometimes I imagine the things you would say
and they make me laugh. Other times I argue with you. Some days
you don't speak at all. Then the dreams come at night with fire and
smoke and my familiar friend, the dead naked man, lying across
the steps of a burnt bakery in Bhendi Bazaar.

I go to a shrink here at the college. I asked her how it is that I
can have nightmares when I wasn't there, never saw any of it. She
says it's called transference and it's coming from my guilt. She says I
shouldn't feel guilty because it wasn't my fault. But she refuses to free
me from seeing her although three years of seeing her hasn't helped
at all with the nightmares.

Anyway, I didn't mean for this letter to get dismal. Overall, I have
had a good time of it in Columbia. I almost think I'm happier here
than I would have been at Harvard. Although that is an impossible
thing to know for certain, isn't it? What life would have been like
if one thing, just one thing had been different. If I step out onto the
road one moment before the light changes (no, I am not suicidal, they
certify it in writing every year). If we hadn't moved from America
to Pakistan. If my father hadn't met my mother. If I hadn't broken
my leg. If the police had never come.

I'm going to pretend now that you're going to write back to me.
That you're going to write and tell me about Xavier's College and your
friends there and your current boyfriend who is a total asshole but
oof the way he looks at you. And that you hate your classes because
they're all full of Boring People and because of that you're quite sure
that I would have loved them.

I probably would have.

Your most Boring Person friend ever,
Tanya

~

*May 1, 1991*
*Karachi*

Dear Tania,

Your letter made me laugh. You're like a spoiled six-year-old. Didn't your father teach you not to throw tantrums? Mine would send me to my room and lock the door every time I cried. Navi also used to throw tantrums when we lived in America but he stopped when we moved to Pakistan. He stopped eating cereal for breakfast when we moved to Pakistan. He also stopped playing baseball and he stopped sleeping in the same bed as me. Just like that.

Yesterday, Chhoti Bibi and I sat down for her first lesson. There is no escaping it: the news is not good.

Her Math is poor although there is a quickness about her because when I ask her basic division questions I can almost see her arranging oranges in a row and calculating the price for half a dozen minus one. Although maybe that's not quickness. Maybe it's just experience in shopping for oranges.

Her English is zero. Her Urdu is just a little better than that and I was treated to an impassioned defence of Punjabi over Urdu. She has a loud voice and she spits.

Her attention span is problematic. After we went through arithmetic, I decided to have a long talk with her about her future and I painted pictures of what her future could look like if she applied herself and got a high school degree, maybe even went to college. She listened to me carefully and I thought she was impressed. I asked her what she wanted to be (bank teller, shop clerk, teacher). She said without hesitation that she wants to be a servant.

It was a blow, I won't lie. But I will persevere. I think with some people ambition has to be taught.

My leg still feels numb. Isn't it supposed to itch by now? You must be wondering why I can't ask my father these questions when he is a brilliant neurosurgeon (the most difficult of all the surgical careers), but it is only because he is so busy building a new hospital in Karachi. This is the reason we moved back to Pakistan, so my father could start a new hospital. We are proud of him.

School closes this week for the summer. I've missed eighteen days of school. If someone had told me even a month ago that I would be able to live through eighteen days of not going to school, I wouldn't have believed it. And now two months of summer. I hate summer. I hate the encroaching ways of the sun, everywhere all the time, impossible to escape.

I hate summer. I really hate summer.

Have you had one of those nights when you can't sleep and even the walls around you begin to seem sinister? Your mind crawls with unhappy thoughts and you begin to obsess over what happened that day. You know, she said, he said but what did he really say, what had she really meant, that sort of thing. And then the most innocent word and the silliest things from the day begin to seem manipulative and cruel and you wonder how you could have been so stupid that you hadn't seen that before. I feel like that. The skin on my back feels so tender, I imagine it sliding off smoothly like the skin of a ripe mango. And there would be my body—all muscles and fat and blood and bone. Nothing like a mango.

Chhoti Bibi was supposed to be here five minutes ago but she is late. I wish she was more like me. The branches of the gulmohur tree outside my window look like mechanical arms, going up and down in the breeze. Before you know it, the evening crows will be here, knocking their beaks stupidly against the glass.

Please tell me. Who is Nusrat?

Best,
Tanya

~

*May 10, 1991*
*Bombay*

Dear Tanya,

You sound DAMN depressed. Good thing I'm punished and can write to you. My mom punished me because I didn't make Distinction in the quarterly exams. I never make Distinction in the quarterly exams. Once my dad even said that to my mom but it didn't make a difference. She just said that Sammy got it every time so I should too. If only I paid attention. If only I focused.

This morning I had another punishment even though it was an invisible punishment. I had to sit next to Anahita Boriwala in Assembly. She is on top of the list of Boring People in the whole school, probably the whole city actually. Her parents made her sign a pledge to only sit in the front row and never, not even by mistake, do anything cool.

Anahita Boriwala smells. Once we were in a play and I was backstage with her and I almost fainted. It's one thing to not be cool but to be uncool AND smelly...control what you can control you know. I am PARANOID about smelling. I smell my armpits at lunchtime every day even though I shower twice a day and use two brands of deo. I tried putting deo down there once for Arjun but it got itchy. Maybe you should also check for Mr Naqvi. I'm just saying it as a friend, don't get mad.

The first thing you need to know about Nusrat is that she's totally normal. If she wore regular clothes no one would be able to tell.

She had an accident when she was a baby and it damaged something in her brain. So she can't speak. She can hear, she can do everything else, she just can't speak. She makes these sounds when she's really excited but that's it. The sounds are really weird.

Her parents are poor-ish. Nusrat works at our house after school, washing the dishes because she wants to save up her own money to get into medical college. She's really, really sure she wants to go to medical college. Her parents didn't want their daughter to work in people's houses but she's like damn stubborn and so finally they had to let her. But she's only allowed to work in our house because her dad built all our furniture and so he knows us like really well.

But anyway, if I ever meet Nusrat's dad and mom I'm going to tell them not to worry because she's DAMN intelligent. I mean I know you're smart but imagine being able to read really fast and write really, REALLY good English when your parents don't even speak it and your mother has only gone to school till the 4th standard and that too in an Urdu-medium school. She doesn't have any siblings which my mother tells everyone at parties as evidence that not all Muslims have lots of kids. And then my father says something mean about Muslims. This is one of their favourite arguments. They also like to argue about drinking, money, how late my mother comes home, how little money my dad makes, my poor grades (whose fault it is), Sammy's money-spending (whose fault it is), the Congress party and this new party that has come up called the BJP or BNP or something.

I tell Nusrat everything. I don't make up good parts. I don't leave out bad parts. When I come home from school and before she has to go home, we go sit by the sea on the rocks where people go to shit in the morning. But it's always clean by evening. The sea takes it away every day.

Nusrat has a notebook and writes in it when she wants to say something. I've asked her to teach me sign language but she says it's silly. I don't know why she thinks it's silly. I mean, do you think it's silly?

Nusrat doesn't like Arjun. I don't want to talk about it.

Yesterday she told me that it wasn't cool of me to ignore Neenee's phone calls. But Neenee calls me four times a day. And when I pick up she gets so excited I just can't help it. I imagine her oily face with all that curly hair (I mean even her moustache hair is curly) and I actually feel the vomit in my mouth. Sometimes I feel like I should tell her. Neenee, don't be so easy. Neenee, wait for me to call you back. Neenee, don't let me make fun of you. But then I hear the happiness in her voice when I call her and I want to slap her.

Neenee is my best friend. We've been friends since we started taking the school bus together when we were in nursery school. She still takes the school bus. I would pick her up in my car on my way to school but her father won't let her. It's really selfish. I mean, just because you're not successful don't make your daughter suffer, right?

At first I thought it was easy to talk to Nusrat because she can't speak. But the thing is when someone doesn't speak, you also speak less. I think words confuse things. Sometimes at school you look around and all the mouths are opening and closing around you and everyone is just talking to talk and you want to stand up and scream at everyone to shut up. Just shut up.

With Nusrat you don't need to say it. You don't need to say anything. You can just sit and look at the sea. She doesn't look at me and I don't look at her. Sometimes we hold hands without looking at each other. With Nusrat, it's damn peaceful.

Love,
Tania

~

*May 20, 1991*
*Karachi*

Dear Tania,

I'm happy to report that there has been some progress from my side. Not a huge amount but definitely, some progress. Baby steps, I say to myself. Chhoti Bibi got 9 out of 10 on a Mental Math test. Granted, it was from a Class III workbook. Granted there was no long division. Still. Baby steps.

I went to tell my mother about it but her door was locked. She's been spending a lot of time in her bedroom except when she is in the garden. She loves plants. Had I told you that? That she loves plants?

The city shut down twice this week because of strikes. I find that short-sighted of our authorities and let's face it, quite rude. What if we had school and had to miss it?

Do you think the passive voice is better for a college essay?

So, is it that you don't want to go to Harvard and Wellesley or is it that you don't want to go to college in America at all? Are you worried that you will miss your family? I can't wait to go back to America. There will be more people like me at Harvard. Plus, my mother's parents live there, of course. We call them Grandma and Grandad. I always feel awkward calling them that which I shouldn't because after all, I am part American. My grandmother wears jeans which is, of course, perfectly normal in America. I suppose I will spend all my college holidays with them. They have a big house. I've spent all my previous summers there. Sometimes when I look up at my grandmother, I find her staring at me. Is it because I'm Pakistani?

I don't really have much else to report so I'll end here.

Best,
Tanya

*June 1, 1991*
*Bombay*

Dear Tanya,
   Did you even read my letter? Here's your Selfish Letter back.

                                                                Tania

~

*June 13, 1991*
*Karachi*

Dear Tania,
   I was going to pretend that I didn't know what you're talking about. But I do. Of course I do.
   Truth: Nusrat made me feel claustrophobic. With her carpenter dad and 4th standard Urdu mum and her adversity and her drive and listening to you on the rocks of the Arabian Sea. She would get into Harvard without even trying.
   And yet it's not just that. I imagined you and her sitting on the rocks of the sea and it was a physical pain in my chest. When we had first moved to Pakistan, my father used to take us to the beach. It was the first place I loved in Karachi although I used to be scared of the waves. My father would laugh at me and hold me up high above his head, the sea around his knees, and I loved feeling his hands banded around my waist, the sky and sea whirling. But we stopped going to the sea. I don't know why. Sometimes I think my father doesn't recognize me when he looks up from his morning tea and sees me at the breakfast table.
   During the monsoons, I like to ask Salim Bhai to drive down that road on my way home from school, even though it

is not on the way at all. He parks near the beach and switches off the engine and we sit there, the rain like a drum on the roof of the car. The windows become opaque and disappear. The sand and the sea merge. I sometimes think this must be what taking a drug is like. To be violently distracted. To not exist momentarily.

You think I am not cool but I am. I always have been but it's only because of my golden hair and white skin which is not even mine, it's my mother's. It's much worse than not being cool because you're plagued by thoughts of how you should be a lot cooler given the deadly ammunition of being white in brown people land but at the same time, you are terrified of waking up one day looking as ordinary as you actually are inside.

People think I'm pretty because when I play hockey my face flushes. My hair shines in the sun. Boys have crushes on me because of it. I just feel hot and silly. As if I'm watching it happen to someone else. Is it not better to be poor but have a space in the world that's meant exactly for you?

You don't have to tell me it's pathetic. I have never been this way. I just need to get out of here so badly. I have nightmares of not getting into college in America and I have nightmares of not getting a full scholarship. I can't afford to go otherwise. Do you understand that kind of pressure? How can you.

I know what people say about hormones and teenagers. But what if it's not hormones? What if we are only just realizing that this is how the world is and that's it, we have to live in it? Half the time I want to stop feeling the things I feel and half the time I'm terrified of what will replace them when I grow up. Of becoming one of the people I see around me, ambling along, blind and deaf to everything that is wrong, everything that can't be explained, everything that is bad and hurts.

Nusrat's story makes her place in the world so very clear. I don't know my place in the world. And I've never understood whether that's because of me or because of the world.

Best,
Tanya

~

*June 15, 1991*
*Bombay*

Dear Tanya,

Dude, that was super intense. Nusrat says to tell you she thinks you're a good writer. I think your sentences are too short and not like pretty. Don't get mad, I'm just being honest.

But I have something super, super important to tell you! Like the most important thing ever! Arjun gave me a ring! Like a real ring! I think it's made of gold. It's got a big diamond. He said it's like a pre-engagement ring because he wants to spend his whole life with me. It was super romantic. We were in his car and it was late at night and it was raining and we were like hugging in the backseat (I had quite a lot of my clothes on) and he just took it out and gave it to me and I started crying and I think even he teared up although I couldn't tell because he's going through this phase where he wears sunglasses all the time. It is the most romantic thing that has ever happened to me.

I have to hide it from my parents because they'd flip out. And I can't wear it to school because rings are not allowed which really sucks because I'm dying to like literally rub it in everyone's face but I can't because he made me promise not to show it to anyone. Haha, he may have stolen it.

Do you think we're like engaged?

I'm going to post this right away so you'll get it faster.

Love,
Tania Malhotra nee Ghosh

PS—Do you think we should meet before I get married?

~

*June 26, 1991*
*Bombay*

Dear Tanya,

I told you Nusrat doesn't like Arjun. I told you that. You don't listen.

Today I had a really deep conversation with Anahita Boriwala. Did I tell you she has no friends? We talked about suicide and parents drinking and wanting to shave off all your hair like Sinead O Connor. She wears two plaits, you know. Even if she hadn't been fat and ugly those plaits would make her ugly. I told her at the end of our conversation that we should talk more but I didn't mean it even in the second when I was saying it.

You're thinking I'm a bitch. Except you're the one using Chhoti Bibi to get into college.

My parents had a big fight today. It sounds like such a cliché but they really have been fighting a lot. I mean, there's always a lot of yelling and shouting in my family but lately it's gotten out of control. My mom says it's because we're intelligent people who enjoy debate but I know she's not talking about me. I'm not intelligent.

I mean she doesn't say it but when she's super mad at me she can't stop herself and she says stuff like she doesn't know what she did to get a daughter like me.

Then my dad gets really mad at her and starts yelling at her and then they forget about me and I go to my room and call Arjun from my own phone line that my Dad got me for my sixteenth birthday. Which my Mom says was with her money. She keeps threatening to disconnect it.

Sometimes when they fight a lot my dad sleeps outside on the couch and sometimes I go and sleep next to him. He puts his arm around me and even though I hate the smell of whisky on his breath, I love how it feels. His stubble tickles me and his arm around me feels like nothing can get to me.

But the last time he made me go back to my bedroom. He said I was getting too old for this. What is 'this'?

My mother locked me into my room which sounds awful but it's such a joke because I can climb the railing of the window and slip out over the top. That's the great thing about being skinny. Other than of course being able to wear whatever I want without bras.

I'm sitting outside right now, writing this. I have Arjun's cigarettes and I am going to smoke all of them so that the box is over because right now the only person I hate more than I hate my mom and my dad is him.

Peace,
Tania

~

*July 2, 1991*
*Karachi*

Dear Tania,
    I don't know how to say this nicely. YOU CANNOT GET MARRIED.

a) You're sixteen and this is illegal. I looked it up. The legal marriage age for girls in India is 18. It's 21 for boys.
b) You can't be okay with his stealing a ring.
c) You have to go to college.
d) What does Nusrat think?

Best,
Tanya

~

*July 14, 1991*
*Karachi*

Dear Tania,

What happened? Why are you angry with Arjun? Did he have to give the ring back to his Mummy? Haha. On a more serious note though, I do hope you're over the engagement fantasy. It's a terrible idea. Just trust me on this.

Your family sounds quite different from mine. No one shouts here. It's quiet.

I thought about what you said about my using Choti Bibi. I disagree. I see it as symbiotic. I am helping her get a better life and she is helping me get a better life. What's wrong with that?

Today I asked her to write an essay on any topic that she wants. Since you love her so much, here's what she wrote. I translated it into English for you.

<u>What I want to be as an adult</u>
*I want to be a maid and look after children in Karachi when I am an adult. I can also be a cook in Karachi when I am an adult. I can also be a gardener in Karachi when I am an adult except*

*I don't want to wear gardener uniforms because I have never worn trousers.*

*I don't want to get married when I am an adult. I want to bring my baby brother Mohammed to Karachi and make him live with me when I am an adult. When I am twenty, he will be eight years old. I will save up all my money and put him in the best school and he will be very clever and he will come first in class and he will only want to eat the food that I cook.*

*I also want to have seven different outfits when I am an adult so that I can wear a different outfit every day.*

*Yours sincerely,*
*Ruksana Mohammed Jamal*

She actually wrote yours sincerely in English and without a single spelling mistake (although her e's are a little hard to decipher). But there you go. That's your beloved Chhoti Bibi. It took her two hours to write this. She's nineteen.

Best,
Tanya

~

July 20, 1991
*Bombay*

Dear Tanya,

I don't give a shit about Chhoti Bibi, I was just pointing out that you were using her. She sounds like a total retard. She probably loves that brother of hers because her mental age is the same as his. She will probably be sold off into someone's house and be made to work like a dog and never get to go home and see her darling brother who will probably die before he grows up anyway like everyone does in our stupid beggar countries. She's so stupid. Seven outfits for seven days. She's dumb.

Most people are dumb. My parents are dumb, my friends are SO dumb.

I've decided I'm not going to college in America. I'm not going to tell my mum but I'm just going to do really badly in the SAT and send in crappy essays.

Today I was really mean to Neenee. Even for me, I was really mean. She didn't even go to the bathroom to cry, she just started crying in front of everyone. It made me hate her even more.

Remember being ten years old? We used to go down to play with water bottles and five rupees to buy spicy sev puri outside the gate of the building which was as far as we were allowed to go. I used to run faster than anyone else and sometimes even after I had caught everyone I used to go on running, running, running. And the wind would be in my hair and the sweat ran down my back and nothing else mattered because I was the fastest runner in the world and I could outrun anyone.

Except of course I didn't. You can't run away from growing breasts and pubic hair. You can't run away from becoming a girl. I hate being a girl. Before we became girls and they became boys it was just about running. You either ran fast or you didn't run fast.

You want to know what happened? Here's what happened. Arjun forced me to go down on him. For twenty minutes. He had promised me after the last time. But today again. Twenty minutes.

Tania

# 3

March 1, 1996
New York, NY

Dear Tania,

There is a poem by T.S. Eliot that we had read for the A Levels.
It started,

> APRIL is the cruellest month, breeding
> Lilacs out of the dead land, mixing
> Memory and desire, stirring
> Dull roots with spring rain.

But you know, I think March is the cruelest month. January and
February are beautiful. Endless flakes that start silently and go on
forever. Like magic everything turns slowly, uniformly, anonymously
blank. Let it snow, snow, snow until I turn softly invisible.

But by March, the snow is gone and the mud is here and everyone
is resentful. The earth is tired of being invisible, we are all tired of
winter wool and chapped hands and the five o'clock dark goes from
cozy to encroaching.

*The weather has been morose since dawn and I have watched it sulk through the window. I have a paper due tomorrow but I can't focus. My mother is not having a good day.*

*My friends say there is a winter Tanya and a summer Tanya which is their way of saying they aren't so fond of winter Tanya. I don't blame them. Summer is so much easier with the sun and the holidays and the new green boughs of trees rubbing up into each other for the first time like new lovers. Isn't it funny that when we lived in similar places I hated summer and you loved it and now I love it and you…hate it? Love it? Are indifferent to it? It amazes me how much I hate not knowing Tania because the entirety of our relationship was really just eighteen and a half months. February 14, 1991 to December 9, 1992. Sixty-seven letters. And yet, your absence like a death.*

*Hey Tania, remember that night you had written to me about when your parents took you and Neenee to buy kebab rolls for dinner and then you drove around Marine Drive afterwards? You pretended to be asleep and your parents held hands.*

*It wasn't all bad. That's the thing with March. With the gray and the cold and the slush creeping slowly into your boots, you remember more the bad parts. But I want to remind you: it wasn't all bad.*

*Love,*
*Tanya*

~

*July 30, 1991*
*Karachi*

Dear Tania,

I've thought about it a lot and I don't know what to say. But for some reason, reading your letter over and over again reminded me of something that had happened when we had just moved to Karachi.

Navi and I had just turned six. My father decided that we should go to Karachi Preparatory. My mother wanted us to go to the American school. But we couldn't afford it so Navi and I both started at Karachi Prep. I'm still at Karachi Prep. Navi was switched to the American School when we were eleven.

Anyway, it's strange what we remember. I remember nothing at all about school. I don't remember Ali, for example, even though he says we were in the same class. I don't remember any of my friends. And yet, I remember clearly that when we came home from school, we used to take a nap in my parents' room which was the only room in the house that had an air-conditioner. We used to wear shorts and nothing else. And even then our skin turned red with heat rash. I remember how the rash looked on my skin. I remember waking up and drinking tepid milk in horrid, dull steel tumblers that had ornate handles with grime on the undersides. I remember picking at the grime and dropping it in my glass so I would fall sick and not have to go to school the next day.

I hated going to school because we were really behind in Urdu even with a tutor coming home to catch us up with the rest of the class. Navi didn't seem to care. But I hated Urdu class. It felt like being deaf, dumb and blind—the script on the blackboard, the drone of poems being chanted that I did not understand. Paeans to Pakistan. It made me feel like a plant. Insensate, stuck in a pot in the corner.

Anyway, one day I was playing around with my tumbler of milk and I spilled it all over the table. I remember it so clearly: the chocolate-coloured milk an expanse of swiftly spreading grey on the glass table and quickly coming to the rim and dripping down onto the floor in loud, fat drops. I remember hating all of it—the table with its stale odour of dirty washcloth, the steam rising from the milk and the drip drip on the floor.

My mother must have heard the tumbler fall because she rushed to the dining room. She saw the mess and—I remember this so clearly—she stepped backwards to the wall and banged her head against it. Once. Hard. Navi and I sat in our chairs and looked at our mother, not crying, not speaking, her head rolling back and forth against the wall, her eyes everywhere but on us. We were six.

I don't know why your story made me think of this except that when I read your letter it took me back to that minute when my mother began to cry. I felt like a clock whose hand had just ticked over and I was irrevocably a new person, a different daughter, a different sister, a different Tanya.

It makes me angry now to remember my mother crying. I was six. Your letter makes me feel the same way. Angry. Helpless.

I don't know if you understand this letter. I'm not entirely sure I do. I know it seems as if it is about me. It's not though. I promise.

Love,
Tanya

PS—I once saw a movie on TV at my grandparents' house in America where the man was pushing down the woman's head, lower and lower, out of the screen. I couldn't tell why she didn't get up and move away. Tell me. I won't say the things you think I am going to say. I really won't.

PPS—I have an update on my leg but we don't have to talk about it right now.

~

*August 9, 1991*
*Bombay*

Dear Tanya,

I guess I was like the girl in the movie. I don't know man it is so hard because you love him so much and really want to make him happy and yet it feels so terrible, like something awful has happened to you. And yet it's not like he hit me or tied my hands and forced me. His hand was on my head and he was gripping it hard. But that's bullshit really because I'm like stronger than him I swear. He's a skinny little piece of shit really. So I don't know. I don't know I don't know. I love him. He loves me, I know he does. Not in school and not in front of people but in private he really loves me. He got me all these condoms the other day you know all in like different colours and said I could pick the one I wanted for when we have sex. He's really sweet like that.

I don't want to talk about it any more.

Love,
T

PS—I didn't mean the things I said about Chhoti Bibi. I hope you didn't tell her.

PPS—I haven't told Nusrat.

~

*August 20, 1991*
*Karachi*

Dear Tania,

My mother came to see me yesterday. She sat with me for a bit. We talked about Chhoti Bibi. She agreed that helping

Chhoti Bibi get a diploma would look good on my applications. I thought I should mention this.

You haven't told Nusrat. Interesting. I was wondering what she would think about it. And no, of course I didn't tell anyone. Do you think I read out your letters at the dinner table?

We don't actually have a dining table anymore. Or rather, it's there but we can't use it as one because it's full of my father's books. He had stacked them there ready to take to his office in the hospital but five months ago, construction stalled.

My father spends a lot of time at the hospital. It's his pride and joy. I think he thought it was going to be all about medicine but from what I understand it's more about money. My father doesn't have much of it. He works very, very hard though. Stays late every night and sometimes he even sleeps there. On weekends I sit with him for breakfast. We don't talk or anything but he reads his paper and I read my book and he lets me serve him his tea.

I don't actually know when my mother eats dinner. I should find out. She has become very thin lately. But she has always been rather slender so maybe I'm just noticing it now since I don't see her every day. You know, because of the knee. Tomorrow I'll find a way to go to her room. I won't be able to ask Chhoti Bibi because of something that has happened but I have resolved to not talk about myself in this letter so I'm not going to even though it was a pretty big thing that happened. A significant thing. A very significant thing. Let me put it this way. School started this week but that is nothing compared to this significant thing.

Yesterday I found a picture of my mother and your mother. It's an old picture. There used to be beads on the frame I remember licking as a child but now most of the beads have fallen off. They are both looking into the camera but they are not smiling. My mother is not as thin as she is now. Her hair is cut short around her face. Your mother's hair is long, black and falling across them both. Your mother's arm is around my mother, her fingers denting the skin on my mother's arm. My mother looks relaxed. If you look closely, her eyes are smiling.

I know when this picture was taken. It was right before my parents' wedding. I know that your mother didn't want my mother to marry my father.

What do your parents look like? My father is short and blockish, like the picture of a boxer he keeps in his study. He has hair coming out of everywhere: ears, nose, arms, legs, neck, even the tops of his hands.

My mother is slim and hairless. She's so tall that she hunches. She's so conscious of being white that she barely goes out. She's so nervous about saying the wrong thing in Urdu that she says very little. My father is not like that. He goes where he wants, he says what he wants, he does what he wants.

Do you look like your mother? Why didn't you tell Nusrat?

Tanya

~

*September 1, 1991*
*Bombay*

I know which picture you are talking about, my mother has it in her study next to a picture of you and your brother from when you were babies. My mom is so bossy it's embarrassing. Why didn't she want your mom to marry your dad? And how is it her business anyway?

Okay so today I told Nusrat everything. Like everything. She didn't say anything. I mean, of course she never says anything but her face went blank the way it does whenever I talk to her about Arjun.

I wish she didn't hate Arjun. I think she HATES him you know? I've tried to get her to actually sit down and get to know him but she refuses. Every time I've made her come into my room, she sees him and gets all stiff and just stares at me the whole time. He even brought her flowers once (well, I bought them and made him give them to her) but she wouldn't take them, she wouldn't even touch them. When he tried to force them into her hands, she dropped them and then looked like she was going to cry.

He's not good with her either. He gets this fake smile on his face and speaks really loudly as if she is deaf. He doesn't get it. Once he said something really rude about her. He doesn't get it.

I wish she wouldn't hate him. I get it though. I would too if I were her.

Today I had a killer day at school so I'm in a damn good mood. I was wearing my new shorts first of all and I got Nusrat to take them in a little bit so they're like really, really short. There wasn't a single boy who didn't look at me. But also I had taken a gamble on one of the new kids in school and it has like TOTALLY paid off. When she joined she was a nobody. But I saw something in her. I took her up—like you know, had her sit next to me a couple of times, invited her out to a couple of parties. So anyway, Nirav, THE coolest guy in my batch, has made her his girlfriend. She's made now. And I did it. And everyone knows it.

It's so much easier to make other people than to make yourself. You work so hard to be the thing you think you want to be and then when you are almost there, you suddenly don't want it anymore. I can't figure out if I get it wrong or if my mind changes.

Does this happen to you?

You know, I don't lie to you. I don't make stuff up when I write to you. It's pretty weird because in school, I lie all the time. I don't lie with Nusrat either but she's different, right? Not the same thing. YOU know.

What's the significant thing with Chhoti Bibi? If it's another Mental Math test I am going to throw up.

Love,
Tania

~

*September 12, 1991*
*Karachi*

Dear Tania,

Your letter made me really happy.

The thing that happened with Chhoti Bibi. I don't know how to describe it. It will sound small and stupid. But she has stopped coming to my room. I haven't seen her in ten days.

I did not know. If I had, I would have done something. I would have told her where to go. I would have sent the driver with her. I would have given her some money. I would have gone with her on my crutches.

I'm lying, I wouldn't have.

It's about jeans.

Chhoti Bibi bought a pair of jeans with her first month's salary. The worst pair of jeans in the world. The kind of jeans you scorn when you see them on people on the street. The kind of jeans heroines in Bollywood movies wore in the 80s. Jeans that we (you and I) would never wear.

Bibi told me later that Chhoti Bibi liked to moon over a picture of me in the living room in which I am wearing jeans. She would tell Bibi every night that she wanted to look like me in that picture. That she wants to wear jeans like mine. Bibi told her that she can buy jeans like that in Karachi. Not true as I have never bought jeans in Karachi but Chhoti Bibi believed her.

As soon as Chhoti Bibi got her first month's salary, she went and bought jeans. I don't know where she went but I can imagine. She was thrilled to buy them and thrilled to show them to me which means something good about me, right? It must mean that I have done something to earn that kind of belief, that kind of trust. She was really excited to show them to me. She was really proud of the jeans. I didn't know that. Should I have known that? I really didn't know that.

The jeans are not even denim. They're cotton with fake denim distress marks all across the fabric. A brilliant blue that will leave bits of dye everywhere. They have pleats. A red stripe running down each leg. Pleats, Tania. You can imagine them, can't you? Please remember that they are not denim.

And I was already angry. She was late. I had been expecting her for almost half an hour. I had prepared a lesson plan. I was bored. I would have been angry with her even if she hadn't been wearing the hideous jeans. By the time she came, it wasn't just the jeans. It was everything. The way she burst into my room, loudly, noisily, waking me up from my evening torpor when I was already half mad with boredom. When it was so hot outside that the sun hurt, bouncing into my room, lighting everything on fire.

She had worn the jeans over her salwar. Oh, terrible, ugly, offensive jeans. They bulged everywhere those jeans, red stripes flashing, cotton stretching. And the salwar…the salwar was orange, a deep, dark brilliant orange, a roomy salwar, not meant to be stuffed into jeans and they took their revenge by spilling out and over the jeans, a big fat bilious orange sausage because Chhoti Bibi is not thin.

And I laughed.

If I could go back now would I take back the laugh? I don't know. Because the truth is I hated her in that moment. I hated her for coming into my room, waking me up, not saying sorry, for thinking she could just do that, just occupy my room and my time. As if she could.

I hated her. The way she looked mortified me. It enraged me. She was wearing a nylon kurta I do not like because it has babies and pineapples on it of equal size. The colours have bled and the edges have blurred so that it looks like a pineapple is swallowing an armless baby. I hate that kurta.

She looked stupid and it made me angry. She was sweating and her hair was plastered on her forehead. She had sweat marks under her arms and her nose and forehead shined with grease.

She smelled of sweat and it filled my air-conditioned room. She was supposed to come and clean the room in the evening, air it out, open the windows, light the candles that I like. Instead she burst in, scattering the used tissues I had thrown on the floor, completely oblivious to me and my feelings.

She looked really stupid. I stand by that.

She ran into my room and skidded to a halt in front of the mirror. She was laughing and sweating and dropped shopping bags on the floor where they spilled sweets, coins and a blue and pink striped handkerchief. She pulled up the baby pineapple kurta and stuck out her hips at me in an effort, I think, to strike a pose like in the film magazines she loves. She wore a yellowed old slip of mine in lieu of a bra, tucked into her orange salwar, tucked into the jeans. Her gaze was not on me, it was on her reflection in the mirror and she looked enchanted by what she saw.

I hated her and I laughed.

At first she didn't move, she didn't even look at me. It was all stillness except for my laughter that fell around the room in waves, the light suddenly turning dimly golden outside like it does in Karachi without notice.

She swivelled her head and looked at me and I noticed suddenly tiny hairs on her smooth brown cheek, the lightest down, turned golden in the light.

Baji, she said. Baji.

I cannot revive the wonder and the hurt in those words. The way she looked at me as if I had hit her. But looking back, I see that even with that wound she didn't shirk, she didn't shrink, no, not Chhoti Bibi. I hurt her and she turned to look me in the eye, her emotions primary-coloured with no shades in between. Baji hurt me. Look at Baji.

She's such a child. Chhoti Chhoti Bibi.

Her hands fell to her sides and her kurta dropped from where she had been holding it up near her chest. It fell halfway, arrested by the bunching of the salwar and the jeans at her waist. She looked worse than before and I felt as angry as before but also, finally creeping in and deflating the anger, shame.

'What?' I said defiantly.

'You don't like the jeans?'

I could not bear the directness of her gaze.

'Throw away the tissues.' I said turning over on my side. 'And pick up your bags. Why did you bring them here?'

She must have stood there and waited for me to turn around for a long time because I saw the sun go down over our garden wall. The leaves turned translucent, opaque and then disappeared into darkness. Finally I heard the door shut and turned around and she was gone. The floor was clean. But there were no candles.

Bibi said she cried all night. And yes, I feel bad about it but Tania…I also feel a weird triumph. I can't explain it. How is it? How is this?

Chhoti Bibi hasn't come to my room in ten days now. Is it over?

Yours,
Tanya

~

*September 25, 1991*
*Bombay*

Dear Tanya,

I just want to say that you are meaner than I am. I am mean to people in my school but never to servants. It's not fair.

The thing is, though, I totally get why you felt good about being a bitch. I feel like that all the time. That's why I can't wait to grow up because I think this must be just a hormones thing. I was totally not a bitch when I was a kid but you know, when you're a kid and you can run fast and your house has cool toys and you don't do anything super stupid in school, it's so easy to be popular. It gets a lot harder when you grow older.

I showed your letter to Nusrat because I think she should know that you have this bitchy side. She didn't seem to think it was that bitchy though. She thought it was funny. She also thinks you're a good writer. Whatever.

So Neenee's mom called my mom and complained about me not being nice to Neenee even though I had TOLD her not to say anything at home. I guess she has been crying again, she's so boring. My mother sat down to have a talk with me about being a better person. She put on her 'I'm a loving parent and my kids can talk to me about anything' face and made me hot chocolate and we sat in the living room (which we never ever do unless there are guests) and she talked to me about being a good friend and a kind person and all this stuff. The whole time I looked at the painting behind her head which is a painting I hate and just swallowed everything I wanted to say because there was a party I wanted to go to that night and I knew that if she felt pleased about being a good mother she would like totally let me go. She's DAMN predictable.

My mom thinks she knows everything but she doesn't even know this about herself. It's pathetic.

But anyway I didn't say any of this because I wanted to go to the party. The lecture lasted thirty five minutes. She didn't even suspect that I wasn't agreeing with her. Thanks stupid, ugly painting I want to burn bit by bit over the kitchen stove.

The party ended up being super lame. Arjun was checking out these eighth standard girls—you know the ones I mean. The ones with the really skinny hips and their boobs just beginning to show.

I'm just so sick of everything. Don't you think there's supposed to be more to life? Than all of this stupid shit? Just more to life. There's got to be more to life. Don't you think?

Love,
Tania

~

*October 5, 1991*
*Karachi*

Dear Tania,

I'm sorry I haven't written in a while. I haven't felt like doing anything really. Not for a few days now.

Things are better with Chhoti Bibi. I've decided to just keep talking to her normally as if nothing has happened. I ask her for advice on things. The other day I asked her to help me rearrange my clothes. I said it out of desperation because I was looking for an excuse to keep her in my room but it was an unexpectedly big hit.

She handles my clothes like they're made of gold. I never thought that t-shirts and jeans and track pants could inspire so much tenderness. She sat in front of my cupboard for hours, stroking and smoothing and folding. I kept up a steady stream of words but then I realized she wasn't even listening.

When she was done and about to leave, I said, 'Sorry.'

She looked at me as if I had slapped her. Then she wrapped her dupatta around her head and left.

I've noticed that she wraps her dupatta around her head when she is nervous or uncertain. Just like Bibi. They both do it when they go outside the house. What security does a dupatta offer? Yet inside the house, they pull up their salwars so you can see their thick legs with sinewy black hair wet from the hot water mop and bucket.

Have you thought about Nusrat applying to college in America? If she really does have good grades and speaks English well and can do well in the SAT, she has a good chance with her story. And perhaps you can help her and that can be your ticket if you're worried about your grades.

Think about it. I think you should do it.

Love,
Tanya

~

*October 16, 1991*
*Bombay*

Dear Tanya,

You do realize that there is more to life than going to fucking college in fucking America right?

Tania

~

*October 27, 1991*
*Bombay*

Dear Tanya,

I want to tell you about my dancing. I haven't told you about my dancing. I am training to do my arangetram in Bharatnatyam this summer. An arangetram is a dance recital. It's like a final exam except you do it in front of everyone like in a concert. Bharatnatyam is supposed to make you very ladylike. My mother did it when she was my age and she's very graceful. Even when she's having dinner at home and not wearing anything special, she looks beautiful. She curls her fingers around the roti and her little finger stands up straight. She sits on the chair like a queen. She's beautiful.

Arjun stares at my mom a lot. She hasn't said anything to me but I'm sure she's noticed it. He's damn obvious. The weird thing though is that she hasn't like forbidden me from seeing him. Her face gets tight when she comes home and sees that he is here. But she hasn't straight out said no you can't date him. My mom is weird like that. She has very clear rules in her head about how the world should work. This is probably because of a rule about letting your children make their own decisions.

My dad hasn't even guessed about Arjun. He has seen him in the house but he just thinks that Arjun is one of my friends. My dad is adorable.

I'm sorry I was rude in my last letter.

Your friends come for your arangetram. Your close friends I mean. I probably won't tell most kids at school about it. I mean I make it sound like a really difficult and beautiful thing you know. It's best to keep it kind of mysterious. I can't tell if it's beautiful. If you lived in Bombay and weren't a BP, I would have invited you to my arangetram.

Love,
T

~

*November 7, 1991*
*Karachi*

Dear Tania,

I got selected as part of the Prefect Group for next year which means I am still on track to be Head Girl. I am up to date on all the school work (although just barely in Urdu) and I will be the captain when hockey season starts again. The only thing I've really lost because of the knee is a shot at the 300 metre swimming record.

I don't dance. And yes, if you don't throw a tantrum every time something annoys you, I would go to your dance recital.

Things are improving with Chhoti Bibi. We've had a couple of conversations but she is still wary of me. I'm trying to be patient.

But I fundamentally disagree with you. You want me to be normal with her because you want to see us interact as equals.

But we're not. I'm at the head of my class and she dropped out of school when she was eight. My parents went to MIT and Wellesley. Her parents are illiterate. I'm going to be a human rights lawyer who works for the UN. She wants to be a servant. I just don't see the point of pretending.

Call me cold and manipulative. I'm just honest.

I talked to my mother about it again. She nodded and agreed with me but I don't know if she was really listening. I think she has a lot on her mind. If she would tell me, I would help her.

It's odd to imagine you doing a traditional Indian dance. Doesn't quite fit in with your talk of sex and tiny shorts and Arjun.

Love,
Tanya

~

*November 15, 1991*
*Bombay*

Dear Tanya,

Whatever man, I'm like super traditional. My mom only wears saris, did I tell you that? I mean a lot of moms only wear saris but most of those moms have always only worn saris. My mom used to wear shorts and bikinis and now she only wears saris. Weird right? Do you think she's going to want me to wear only saris when I'm her age?

My brother called early this morning so everyone's in a damn good mood. He said he loves Princeton and was telling me about his eating club which sounds pretty gay to me but he says everyone does it and that it's like a fraternity. Frats scare me. The thought of all those white boys with blonde hair and beer. What would it take to make them like a brown girl?

You know, this is the first time my brother has called that he sounds like his old self. It has taken a year.

Last night, Neenee came over and we all went for a drive on Marine Drive. First we stopped and got frankies which are the most awesome kebab rolls except they don't have kebabs in them. We ate the frankies in the car and then after dropping

Neenee home we went for a long ride in the car. I closed my eyes and pretended to be asleep. When we got to Marine Drive, my dad stopped the car and rolled down his window and bought cigarettes for my mom. My mom only smokes when she's really happy and she thinks that no one can see her.

My dad switched on the radio to a station that plays old Hindi movie songs. They both love old Hindi movies. My mom put her hand on my dad's leg and my dad put his hand over hers. After a while the traffic died down and you could only hear the music and the sound of the waves outside. If they were quiet all the time they would never fight.

I haven't told my brother about Arjun. He doesn't think I should have a boyfriend even though he has always had a girlfriend for as long as I can remember. I really liked the last one but he broke up with her before going to college. She should have tried harder.

Love,

T

~

*November 25, 1991*
*Karachi*

Dear Tania,

A lot has happened. I don't even know where to start. Two boys in my class got kidnapping threats.

I know both the boys quite well. One is the younger brother of a boy I know well, Mustafa; we call him Musti. The other is not in my class but I know him because we did inter-school debates together.

Musti is the class clown. He is perpetually on the brink of

failing out of our class altogether. He is one of those people who has been part of the class since lower KG. He is in all the birthday party pictures from way back when the boys used to wear tight shorts and the girls wore frilly dresses in green and pink and cream.

I called Musti. He didn't sound scared at all. A bunch of the boys were over at his house and I could hear them laughing in the background as if it was a big joke. I asked Musti what was going to happen to his brother but he didn't know.

The worst part is that Ali is in London. He has been gone for a week. A show his parents are producing. It took me an hour to get Ali on the phone. He hadn't heard the news. I guess it's not big news in London. He has missed a week of school and his family just doesn't seem concerned. I am keeping notes for him and I've arranged for Shaishta to keep notes for him for the two classes I don't have with him but even though he said thank you very nicely I don't think he really cares.

The thing is, Ali's family is very rich. Richer than anyone else I know. They have a house in London and a house in New York and many houses in Karachi. His parents do theatre and film and are very intellectual. I guess they can afford to be because both his parents' families own most of Pakistan. They spend their summers in London. Now they're thinking of moving there. I don't understand families like that. How do you just decide to move to London like that? How can it be so easy? Leaving Boston was the biggest thing that has ever happened to my family. We still haven't recovered from it. But Ali's family is like that. They are all very vague. Maybe his father thought Ali might get better music there. Maybe his mother thought British school uniforms are better looking. You never know with Ali's family. They're vague.

They don't even have bodyguards. People who are far less wealthy keep bodyguards. Why can't they be like normal rich people and have bodyguards?

I know you think I am cold and calculating. But Ali has to come back. When he smiles everything is fine even though I know that his smile is not just for me.

I told him he has to come back. He said, 'Don't worry, I'll come back.' But that sounds ambiguous. When will he come back? Will he come back for good or just to get his things? I was too scared to ask. He said I was stressed and played me a song on his guitar that he had heard someone play on the street. It sounded familiar but I couldn't place it and now it is playing in the back of my head, insistent and soft and impossible to trace.

Love,
Tanya

# 4

March 23, 1996
New York, NY

Dear Tania,

900 people died in the Bombay riots between December 6, 1992 and 19 January, 1993. Two years ago, 800,000 Rwandans died. 6 million Jews died in the Holocaust. 3 million people died in the Bengal famine of 1943. 20 million Russians died in World War 2.

900 people.

This feels like old times, though, doesn't it? Taking pen to paper, saving up what to say and then parsing carefully so that only the best remains. Did you know that every letter I wrote to you was first written in draft sometimes twice, even thrice? The final I would write with a beating heart on letter paper stolen from my father's study. And then I'd get your letters, scratched out words and overwritten sentences with arrows pointing to corners of pages where you had another thought. Fido Dido and Donald Duck idly leaning on the edges. Your first letter was on the back of a grocery list. I know it by heart. Two kilos of potatoes, one kilo of tomatoes and one kilo of onions. Cornflakes, baking powder and repair Shayon's Titan. I spent hours imagining what a Titan could be (sword, armour, breastplate) until Mala told me it's a brand of wristwatch.

*I was telling Jake about it. He has big shoulders and I tried
having sex with him last summer. It was not great. My friend Jodie
loves sex and she's not making it up because I hear her through the
wall. You loved sex too. I don't understand it. Maybe it would help
if Jake didn't chew with his mouth open.*

*But still, it's so different from what I had imagined, what I still
imagine. I must be the only person in the world who enjoys the
imagining of it more than the doing of it. Had I ever told you about
the first time I fantasized? You will laugh because it was to a book.
The Darling Buds of May by H.E. Bates. It was full of big breasts
and cheery men and happy families. I rubbed myself against page
67. It was marvellous.*

*I know what you're thinking: Adventures of Tanya the Boring
Person. Say it. Say it to me. Call me on the phone and call me stupid,
call me boring, call me cold, call me cruel, call me selfish, call me
something, call me anything.*

*I sometimes imagine that I'm going to pick up the phone and call
you in the middle of the night because that will be the only time to
catch you before your morning classes and then I'll tell you all about
the sex I had last night and you'll laugh at me and tell me that I
should really let him do that because oof it's so much fun if only I
would stop being such a tightass about it.*

*I must admit that it's nice to be held. I never had nightmares
with Jake. He's gone now.*

*Did you know that the Partition was the largest peacetime
migration of people in the written history of the world? 12 million
people crossed the border. 1 million died. 75,000 women were raped.
I often wonder how they calculate these numbers. Did they go around
asking the women? What do they ask? What are the words they use?
Do they talk about shame?*

*Is that what drove you that day? The fear of men? The fear of shame?*

*I once had a toy camera on a keychain. It was one of those
cameras where the pictures are pre-loaded and every time you clicked*

a new picture would show up in the viewer. Except something was wrong with this camera. The moment you opened the fake shutter, it would just start clicking away by itself, picture after picture flashing and the whole thing would grow faster and faster until it's just a whir and you can't see anything. Click. Click. ClickClick. Cliclick. Cliclick.

It's like that with me now. I see trains of dead people and pieces of bodies and staring, desolate women in white saris wandering through empty buildings. But how can it be because I was born 27 years after Partition. We never studied it in school. My father's parents are both from Karachi. My family was not part of it, did not suffer. I never heard a single story. There is no reason for my nightmares.

If anything, the nightmares should come to you. But I'm sure they don't dare.

Sometimes I think Pakistan is my mother, your mother, both our mothers together. Impossibly tender one minute, carelessly cruel the next. We talk too much, we talk about everything. We talk too little and we are silent. Words hurt and then the absence of words hurts. Everything hurts. Remember how we had talked about that? And we both thought it would be different when we grow up.

We come from a bullshit people. My therapist calls it transference but I'm not transferring anything that is not somewhere mine. It's somewhere yours too, Tania. You can ignore my letters, you can ignore my phone calls like you ignored the phone call Chhoti Bibi made to you when I was in the hospital for mad people. But it didn't just happen to you. It happened to me. It happened to me. You keep pretending like it only happened to you but it happened to me. It happened to me.

Love,
Tanya

*PS—I might as well tell you. My other major is Political Science. I'm studying the rise of religious extremism in the sub-continent. My thesis is on the Bombay riots.*

~

*December 9, 1991*
*Bombay*

Dear Tanya,

Wow. Your life suddenly got interesting. Kidnapping threats. Your boyfriend in a British school blazer. Sexy. When are you sending me his picture?

It's so boring here. We don't get any kidnapping threats. The most exciting thing that is happening here is that there's a cross-country chariot race going on. Although I don't see how it's a race because there's only one chariot and even that you can tell is really just a regular bus that they've made into a chariot.

I don't even know why this is such big news because it looks like a comic book come to life you know—a lot of bright colours and people playing dress up and carrying around swords and spears and stuff.

But everyone is talking about it. That's all you hear on the news. My parents' fights have new life and they're both full of energy and new information. Did you know Aurangzeb did this bad thing? Did you know Akbar did this good thing? Why are you so blind? Why are you so prejudiced?

There's a guy called Advani and he says that we should stop apologising for being Hindu. He's got a point, why should we apologise for being Hindu? I'm not going to. Except I've never actually heard anyone apologise for being Hindu.

I asked my mom why he's doing a chariot race and she said it's because he wants to destroy a mosque in a place called Ayodhya (which is where the god Ram was born and I thought it was made up but my mom says it's a real place which makes everything about Hinduism so confusing.) My dad said that there used to be a really important temple there to begin with and that Babar had destroyed it and built a mosque in its place. He said that of course he can't expect her to tell me the whole story and that she's a pseudo secularist. He said that the Congress has destroyed the country and it's time for new blood. My mother said that the BJP is only going to be good for rich people but she said it in an angry way as if we're not rich. My father got up and left the table without finishing his dinner.

What does it mean to be pseudo secular? We say pseudo in school when someone is being fake. I mean my mom is fake about a lot of things like I've told you before. She says it's the most important thing to be a good person but really she means a rich, successful person because otherwise she wouldn't be so mad at my dad all the time.

I've never really thought so much about religion. So I guess the BJP is good in that sense because they're making you think about this shit. But I don't get why everyone is so excited about the historical stuff. It's pretty boring.

My mom is damn political. She's always mad because we don't talk about politics in school. Whatever, we're like practical. We talk about money.

There's a guy in school, Rahul, who is sort of my friend. He totally supports the BJP. He says it's going to be good for business. I swear, when he's not stoned Rahul sounds like a Gujju businessman. I mean that's what he's going to be when he grows up because that's what his dad is. Thank God my dad never pressures me to become an accountant. The next time I fight with my mother, I'm totally going to say, 'Dad never pressures us like you do!' Ha. I can see her face now. Her mouth will be slightly open, her eyes will bulge a bit like they do when she's angry. It will be AWESOME.

Anyway I'm all for a new party to be in power you know. It HAS to be better than what we have. You know apparently we were almost bankrupt over summer and had to send two planes of gold to Switzerland or something to beg for money. I never want to beg for anything.

My mom asked me yesterday what I want to be when I grow up and I said, rich. And she said that I have a much better chance of becoming rich if I go to Wellesley. If I told her that I wanted to marry Arjun and have babies she would tell me that going to Wellesley will make me better at having babies. I don't think she thinks it's possible for me to become a person without going to Wellesley.

How come your mom isn't like that? I mean they are best friends. Did you see how they talked on the phone for like an HOUR last weekend? And I get lectured on the phone bill when I called Arjun when he went to see his dad in Delhi! I mean he was CRYING.

Things are really good with Arjun. His dad just closed a big deal so he's like totally happy with Arjun which means that Arjun is totally happy with me. He gets kind of mean when his dad is mean to him. We had the best kiss ever the other day behind the school where the Siddharth College students go to pee. I told him I want him to kiss me like that at Nirav's party and he laughed. Do you get the joke?

Do you think we should talk on the phone?

Ciao,
Tania

*December 19, 1991*
*Karachi*

Dear Tania,

I don't think my mother even knows which year of school I am in. Do you know when my leg was broken she came to see me four times? Her bedroom is seventeen steps from mine. She didn't come to the hospital when they were setting it. She probably thought my father was going to be there.

Navi says to leave her alone. She IS alone. She spends all of her time in the garden fussing over the orchids as if they are newborns. I didn't know she had talked for an hour on the phone with your mother. I didn't know she could talk for an hour. Are you sure it was my mother?

In case you haven't noticed, your life is a little different from mine. While you sit around machinating and scheming about boyfriends and social power, the boys I have grown up with are getting death threats. In school these days, we all get nervous when a boy is absent. Musti's parents have decided to send Musti and his brother to boarding schools in the UK. They are in the UK now, looking at schools. There are rumours everywhere.

No one can fully explain the kidnappings, although our political parties are blaming each other. Natasha said she is going to write her college essay about sectarian violence in Pakistan. It sounds like a good idea on the face of it but I think it's too superficial. It's like a black student in America writing about racism. No, I think they are looking for deeper thinking than that. But Natasha's dream school is Carnegie Mellon so it doesn't matter what she writes.

I almost got angry with Ali today. We were all at Fati's house and he was playing Fati's guitar in the balcony with a boy we don't know, smoking expensive foreign cigarettes. Apparently Ali had brought him to Fati's house. I asked Fati to say something but she just shrugged and said, 'Chill.'

I dislike it when people say that. If you can't say something useful Fati, it's often better to say nothing at all.

I called Ali inside and spoke to him about it. He just patted me on the back and said, 'Don't worry Tanya. He's not going to kidnap me.'

How does he know? As if kidnappers politely let you know their intentions in advance. Maybe we shouldn't go to Fati's house anymore. I want to tell Ali that but either he will laugh at me or he will nod with grave, sincere eyes and forget all about it the next minute.

Sometimes I think Ali only comes into our world some of the time. Even Chhoti Bibi gets impatient with him. Even when I talk about him to Chhoti Bibi I can tell that she gets impatient. 'He started singing in the middle of class Baji?' 'He forgot to call you again Baji?' 'Did his parents decide about their moving to Ingyland Baji?'

I don't know Chhoti Bibi! I don't know! I really don't know and the worst part is he doesn't seem to care! As long as he has his beloved music and cricket I don't think he would even notice if he got kidnapped.

I've sent off my requests for college applications. Ten. I'm going to pick six. It will be hard but I can do it. Have you sent off your requests for college applications? You better do it soon. The other night I dreamt that Harvard had forgotten to include the application and I discovered it the day before I had to send it.

Are we going to tell each other which colleges we are applying to? I will if you will.

Love,
Tanya

PS—I can't call you. It's too expensive.

~

*December 28, 1991*
*Bombay*

Dear Tanya,

You know, every time I begin to like you, you bring in all the college stuff. Can you like not do that? You're a bit obtuse about taking hints. I'm telling you as a friend.

I think your brother is wrong about your mother. She's definitely being weird. I thought twin brothers would be different. I had always thought that if Sammy had been my age he would have taken me seriously. But I can't see Sammy as anything but Sammy. Head Boy, School Sports Captain, going to Princeton, everybody-loves-him, two dimples that trick everyone into not noticing that he's already balding.

Nusrat thinks it's really crazy what's going on in Karachi with all the kidnappings. I mean I do too obviously. But she's like obsessed. These days as soon as she's done with the dishes she comes to my room with all these papers that she buys from the raddiwala—English, Hindi, Marathi, Urdu, even Gujurati. And she cuts out all the articles on Karachi. It's kind of annoying, she covers my room with all the cuttings and keeps going on and on about it in her notebook and ignores all my hints. I tune out and just look at her. I like how she looks when she's excited about something. Her eyes get super big. Her braid slips from one shoulder to the other until she gets annoyed and pins the whole thing up like a pineapple behind her head. She looks nice in white. Like really nice.

Today I was telling her about how Arjun was nice to me in school and she wasn't even listening. She said sorry and stuff but I mean whatever. I can't wait for her to get bored of this stuff.

I asked Arjun again why he can't be my boyfriend in school. He just hugged me and kissed me and said he loves me. Is that an answer, Tanya? I wish I was clever so I understood without having to ask anyone.

Love,
Tania

PS—Nusrat can't help it because she has family in Karachi. Like second cousins. Maybe you could send some Karachi newspapers. I think she'd really like that. Then maybe she'd stop being so selfish and listen to my stuff again.

~

*January 11, 1992*
*Karachi*

Dear Tania,

I have enclosed five newspapers for Nusrat. I've underlined the relevant articles.

I almost wish I understood you and your ambitions. Wanting your mother's approval I understand (although I understand very well her ambition for you). I don't understand your burning ambition to be Arjun's girlfriend. And how is the girl you had 'made'? Is she grateful to you? What if she isn't nice back? You didn't even know her.

It just seems so exhausting. I always feel so relieved when I'm home from school in my own room with my books and pictures on the walls and my desk the way I left it. Some days I want to come home from the first period of school. I'm not sure I like people.

I'm having some trouble with Ali. He's really upset with me. He's never been upset with me before. Part of me thrills to it.

We have exams in school and the only way I can do well in Urdu is to learn everything by heart. Ali wanted me to go to a Nusrat Fateh Ali Khan concert with him. Of course I wanted to, but my father says that one has to make sacrifices for one's goals and my goal is to get the highest marks in every subject in these exams and you know, Urdu is hard for me.

I told Ali that I couldn't go because I had to learn all the poems by heart. He didn't say anything but that evening he came to my house…and you have to promise not to ever say anything about this to anyone…with the Urdu exam paper.

Of course I didn't. I tore it up and threw it away, in fact. But Ali just didn't understand why I wouldn't just look at it. 'If you know what's on the paper, then you only have to learn what's on the paper and then you can come with me to the concert.' He looked so hurt.

You have to keep this in the strictest confidence because this could destroy his chances of getting into a good college. It could destroy his life. But I'm so distraught about it that I have to tell someone.

Is he a dishonest person and I just didn't see it? Only cowards cheat after all. Right? But Ali never even lies. Sometimes I wish he would lie and tell me that the phone was busy instead of saying he forgot to call me or worse, that he hadn't felt like it. He either does really well or really poorly in school. If he cheats, wouldn't he do well in everything?

I was very angry with him, Tania.

And for the first time since I've known him, he got angry back. He said that he was trying to support me in what I love and that I don't support him in what he loves.

What does he love? A concert? One that he's not even playing in!

Maybe it is not Ali, maybe it is me. I don't understand men. I don't understand my father. I don't understand my brother. Today my father was home for dinner because a surgery was cancelled (the patient died). He, Navi and I had dinner together, a silent meal. I told him, although he didn't ask, that my mother was sleeping. He nodded. I said it again in case he hadn't heard me and he said, 'I heard you Tanya. Your mother is sleeping.'

How can he not think it is strange that she's sleeping at nine o'clock at night when her children and husband are sitting down to dinner?

I forced Navi to look at me and I saw that he had registered it, registered all of it. But he turned away from me and talked about muscle atrophy with my father for the rest of the meal. Sometimes I think he doesn't like to be around me because he doesn't want to accept reality.

But at least I know that he sees it too. The ever-increasing strangeness of our mother. I almost never see her anymore. She's hiding. She's shrinking. She spends all day in bed and at night, when the gardener has gone home, she floats around our garden in a thin nightie, fondling roses and stroking dew from leaves. One morning I found her curled around a baby jacaranda bush. Once I heard her singing lullabies to the jasmine. The lullabies she used to sing to me.

There is a memory I have of being a child when we had first moved to Karachi. We had gone to my father's friend's house, his mentor from college I think. The house was musty and the couple seemed impossibly old. I remember Navi had started crying and my father had looked at him with such annoyance on his face that I knew he had forgotten he had brought us with him. My mother picked us up, one in each arm and that must have been hard because we were at least five years old. She took us out to the garden where it was fresh and cool and she stayed outside in the garden with us the whole time even when my father came outside to call us in to eat. I remember that scene as if it is a picture, the light fading over the champa trees and fat waxy flowers falling all around us as if something had died.

I would try to answer your question about why Arjun doesn't want to be your boyfriend but why would you want advice from a girl whose family didn't even notice the big silver cup she won and left by the staircase for everyone to see?

Love,
Tanya

P.S. Besides, Tania, you already know.

~

*January 22, 1992*
*Bombay*

Dear Tanya,

Your letter made me sad man. And then I felt like an asshole for being stressed about something stupid like not being invited to a birthday party.

I'm joking. Of course I'm invited to the party. I'm invited to every party. It's not even a party if I'm not there. Everyone says that because it's absolutely true.

Your mom sounds weird. She also sounds sad. Why isn't your dad noticing?

My dad is really good at noticing things. Actually, he notices things a bit too much. He's too sensitive. I tell him this all the time when he's sad after a fight with my mom. I tell him to chill and have a cigarette. It's a joke because once he caught me smoking and instead of scolding me, he started laughing and then we both laughed and laughed and laughed and I fell over and that made us laugh even more and finally when we stopped laughing he didn't say anything to me about smoking and instead we both promised not to tell my mother.

Sometimes I have a fantasy about my mother not being there. Maybe going to visit Sammy for a long, long time. And it will be just my dad and me.

Today I did something stupid at school but I don't care. We have this thing where every week we go do stuff for the poor. It's really boring and stupid because I always go to the Soup Kitchen with the rest of my gang because it is run by Laila's mother. But there's never anyone there at the Soup Kitchen at the time that we go because that's a super busy time for beggars. Today—I don't know what came over me—I went to St. John's Church instead where they also give food but it's to street kids. And the kids were actually there.

I mean they were disgusting and dirty and super rude but at least they were there. It was super tiring because we had to serve them food and then give them these tiny bars of soap and make them go take showers and stuff.

When I came back to school, everyone was giving me weird looks and Maya made a face as if I smelled. So I was like, how was Gossip at the Soup Kitchen today? But no one laughed.

At that moment, I didn't care. I just went and played tennis and beat everyone I was so mad.

But now I'm home and I'm tired and I've eaten dinner and it's 10 pm and no one has called me all evening. That's like never happened.

But why can't I go to St. John's? Why does everyone have to be together all the time? I mean is our group so fragile that if someone does something different then it's all over?

See this is why I feel like growing up is so dangerous. I never used to think this kind of stuff before. Now I feel like everything is stupid and everyone is stupid. This is the kind of thinking I don't want to do. It's dangerous.

My dad once told me that growing up feels like shedding your skin and growing new skin. Well, I like my old skin a lot. It took a lot of hard work to grow it and I don't want anything else. I'm scared I'm going to become a Communist like my parents used to be. They used to like sing songs on the streets and be against everyone. I don't want to be like that. It's hot and sweaty and you can't look cute doing it.

Besides if you're against everything then who runs things? Where does the money come from?

Do you sometimes feel like you're shedding your skin? I think I'm going to pray tonight and ask God if I can keep mine. And maybe see if he can send my mom on a holiday.

Love,
Tania

~

*February 1, 1992*
*Karachi*

Dear Tania,
You won't believe what just happened. Just as I was going to sit down to write to you, there was a huge crash in the kitchen. When I went to see what it was, I found Bibi pinned to the floor by a huge steel cupboard that had fallen down on her. Chhoti Bibi was standing there, arms folded across her chest, looking mutinous.

I helped Bibi up and she cursed away in Punjabi involving all manners of animals in interesting combinations with Chhoti Bibi's ancestors and my ancestors even though I had done nothing but try to help her.

As soon as Bibi was free of the cupboard, she sprung up and slapped Chhoti Bibi hard across the face. Once, twice, thrice. Before I could move. Chhoti Bibi just stood there looking straight at Bibi. She didn't try to defend herself and she didn't try to stop Bibi. The slaps were hard and her cheek was already swelling up but there were no tears in her eyes. She just stood there blazing at Bibi. It got very quiet.

Then Chhoti Bibi swore and walked out. I was left standing there with Bibi who began to cry. I helped her to her room and made her lie down. I got some balm for her bruises. Her pillow turned wet under her cheek, her wrinkles forming rivulets. I've never seen Bibi cry before.

It turns out that there was a marriage proposal from their village for Chhoti Bibi. Of course this is a huge thing because no one ever thought Chhoti Bibi would get married after what she did to the first guy. But Bibi had been sending home a lot of money and finally they had found a family with a boy who is slightly retarded.

I think Bibi genuinely thought Chhoti Bibi would be happy. It's amazing how little families actually know each other.

I went outside to look for Chhoti Bibi but couldn't find her anywhere. The gardener said she took off by the back exit and my old bicycle is missing. At first I thought it was funny—Chhoti Bibi in her huge salwar biking away angrily on a pink and white bicycle with My Little Pony handlebars. But it has been a few hours now and it is almost dark and she is not home.

I'm sure she's fine. She's a smart girl. And she's been in the city for a few months now. She knows our address. She must know it because she goes to buy groceries in the car with Bibi. She can be flighty sometimes though and I wonder if she paid attention. Knowing her, she was probably so thrilled to be in an air-conditioned car, she hadn't noticed. And really, it has only been four months. Would I have known Clifton if I had only lived here for a year and that too as a servant? What if she has left Clifton? She has an unknowable number of cousins around the city in neighbourhoods I don't know, whose names I only read in newspapers when bad things happen.

I'm sure she's fine.

Love,<br>
Tanya

~

*February 15, 1992*
*Bombay*

Dear Tanya,

Today I got into a fight at school because stupid Aparna said I have no school spirit and I said fuck school and a Prefect was walking by, a total chaap who has never heard of shampoo or deodorants, and he said he was going to give me detention. I mean please. Prefects aren't allowed to give detention, get a life! I told her that and she said, come with me right now come to the Principal's office and I said make me and he actually grabbed my hand and tried to pull me but whatever I'm super strong and I burst out laughing and some spit landed on his arm and now he's saying I spat on purpose. I have to talk to Ms. Kuruvilla tomorrow. Basically, I'm not getting Prefect next year.

I came home and cried to Nusrat. She was so nice about it. I put my head on her lap and she put her arms around me and made those noises that she makes when she feels something a lot. She smelled really nice and her hands on my face were so cool and smooth and soft. How is it that she's poor and doesn't smell? I mean I'm not being a bitch, poor people don't have money to buy deo. If I forget my deo for a day I smell. Nusrat is magic.

I told my mom and she said that it didn't matter because American colleges don't care about Prefects.

I want to go to Xavier's College and study Psychology and then I want to have a big wedding where I'll wear a tiny choli with a huge red ghaghra with gold all over it and dance on stage and everyone will be looking at me, even the gross fat uncles but no one will be able to say anything because it will be my wedding.

And then Arjun and I will have our own house where I will paint the walls interesting colours and have sex everywhere. Arjun will do damn well in his business and I'll be the hottest married woman in Bombay and I'll wear whatever I want all the time and no one would be able to stop me because I'll be married.

I was mean in school today. Just regular stuff, stuff I've always done. But it's bothering me. I convinced Maya that Sunil has a crush on her and that she should go talk to him. And she did and he got up and walked away. And everyone saw and started laughing. And Maya is no dumb fool you know so she also started laughing and made a big joke out of it.

But she wouldn't look at me afterwards.

And the fucked up thing is that this would have never bothered me before.

That's what I'm saying man. I like my skin. I don't want it to change. I never thought about this shit before and I don't want to start now.

I guess Chhoti Bibi had to get away for a bit. I can just see her cycling away on your old pink bicycle, wanting to get away from your house, from your stupid lesson plans, from Bibi, from everything. I mean if I didn't have a boyfriend, if I didn't have Arjun I would totally want to get away. But I have Arjun and he's the hottest boy in school and he loves me so I have no reason to want to get away. My life is awesome. I'm happy. I'm like totally happy.

Love,
Tania

## 5

April 5, 1996
New York, NY

Dear Tania,

Today I saw the first daffodils! Real daffodils growing in the ground, beautifully yellow and pristine and rising above the muddy leftover snow. They reminded me of gulmohurs in Karachi. Karachi doesn't have spring but around the time that it was going to be the end of the year and everyone was slacking off in the classroom and the teacher wasn't really trying, we used to stare out of the window at the gulmohur tree in the basketball court, especially on that magic day when it seemed like it had bloomed overnight. One day just a normal sober tree and the next day a party. I always thought the tree lived through the whole year just to have those flowers.

It is hard to have relationships with trees here. Other than in the park, most of New York's trees are chained up in fences. There are cherry blossoms by the reservoir though and they, like the gulmohurs of Karachi, come alive suddenly and vividly in spring. All year long, I run round and round the reservoir, imagining every pound I've eaten drop cleanly off my body but in spring I don't even care. In spring, the cherry blossoms triumph and for a few days, all longings are met in paper-thin, pink and white whispers blowing perfume into the air.

You always made sex sound so easy.

I'm angry with you for that. I'm angry with you for a lot of things actually.

For a long time I was angry with you for having sex with Arjun, for letting him do all those things to you. There was something so absolute with you about Arjun. You were just so sure. It set an impossible standard. It still does. Every time I have approached a relationship, I have pictured you in my head, imagined what you would have said. I compare how I feel to how you had felt about Arjun. Your love was singular, full and fecund. Mine sterile and stillborn.

But I don't feel angry with you about Arjun anymore. I think everyone has to have one obsession in their life. Something that grabs you by the ankle and swings you around the axis of the world until you become a doll, chucked into the universe, whirling, whirling, gone.

Yes, I think so. I don't think we die once in a lifetime. Sometimes in one life itself we die many times. I took a class on Hindu philosophy and I think that's what reincarnation is really about, shedding the angst and pain of a lifetime so you become thinner, cleaner, simpler, smaller.

Arjun was your obsession. It was clear from the way you talked about him. His crazy body, his crazy mind, the crazy way he loved you, his hands on your buttocks, his hands in your hair, his hands on your feet, his hands on your mouth holding it shut while he fucked you. You were obsessed. I understand now. I'm not angry anymore because I understand.

Winter is almost over. This morning I woke up and opened the window and jumped out into the garden and it was soft and secret and dreamy. I imagined a gentle knight and a sorrowful princess and he was smiling at her with all the patience in the world. The knight *was my father and the princess was my mother. They began to touch each other and did not notice me hiding under a rosebush. And I, absorbed as I was in watching them did not see you, writhing with a snake in a pit right next to me. The snake rose up and struck you and you fell forward dead in the sand, looking straight at me with a smile on your face.*

*This is a nightmare I've had for three and a half years. Well, there are versions. Sometimes there's no snake, it's a gun. Sometimes there's no noise at all as if it's happening in mute. Once, in the dream, I was blind but I could still feel you fall. Every time you fall with a smile on your face watching me.*

*It didn't just happen to you. It happened to me, Tania, it has never stopped happening to me.*

*Love,*
*Tanya*

~

February 25, 1992
Bombay

Dear Tanya,

Okay that was less weird than I thought it was going to be. You sound a lot more normal on the phone. Except you have a weird accent. But I'm glad I called.

It was pretty crap that you didn't write and tell us that Chhoti Bibi was back. You know I made the maid wait outside for the postman for two weeks. And it's like really hot outside. You're INCONSIDERATE.

Chhoti Bibi sounded fun although I didn't understand a lot of what she said. You know what Tanya, I think inside, below the crappy stuff that comes from being poor, she's actually cool.

Cooler than you. It makes me sad actually. There are so many people who would have been total social rockstars and they can't because they're poor. It's over for them before they even have a chance.

It was kind of tough for Nusrat. I kept trying to give her the phone because you know she can like make some noises but she wouldn't take it. She can be shy. She does sound weird so maybe it was good she didn't. I'd be pretty mad if you said the wrong thing to her.

So anyway the big update from my side is that Sammy has a girlfriend and she's BLACK. She's from NIGERIA. Yeah. Insane. I mean I think it's weird that he couldn't get an American black girl to date him. My mom forbade him to go to Nigeria because it's like super dangerous. He told my parents that she's super smart and is at Princeton on a full scholarship. He told me she's hot like a model.

If I wasn't so short I'd be hot like a model. I have the Bengali eyes you know? Except they're normal big on me not like protruding big like they are on some people (my mom).

I have a nice ass and REALLY hot legs. My problem is my boobs. They keep growing man. I mean I know it sounds sexy and stuff but I don't want it to get to the point where they are like Anjali's, I mean she can't even run and she can NEVER wear tank tops. I already can't wear tank tops without a bra which is so sexy you know. Like a plain simple white tank top over jeans right after you've shampooed your hair and your skin is soft and shiny and just slightly sweaty, I mean sometimes I look so hot in the mirror I can only imagine what it does to guys.

How much hotter do I have to be for Arjun to love me in public? He was mean to me today.

Do you think it ever gets simple? I think it used to be simple at one point for my parents. My dad has told me stories about how they met and how they fell in love. You know my mom like totally stood up for him to her parents. They wanted her to marry someone rich like them. And my mom was like I'm going to marry this guy or no guy. And it worked.

I mean I think that's cool but I wonder if she would have married him if my grandparents hadn't been against it, you know. What if she was trying to prove to herself that she was powerful, that what she wanted mattered more than what they wanted? What if that's the reason she married my father? Is that good enough?

What makes someone good enough? What is a good enough reason to want to spend your life with someone?

Love,<br>Tania

~

*March 3, 1992*
*Karachi*

Dear Tania,

It was nice of you to phone us. Chhoti Bibi couldn't stop talking about it for days. You have become her hero. 'No one has ever called me from India before,' she kept saying. 'All because I went to my cousin's house.'

It must be nice to be able to pick up the phone and call anyone you want without worrying about the expense.

Remember I had told you I need to look over the family finances? Today I found the door of my father's study unlocked after a long time. It was dusty inside and smelled of the petrified black thing in the dustbin that had been a banana a long time ago. I also found the folders I was looking for. My father's bank statements.

Things are worse than before. My father has sold his last remaining investments. There has been no income for over a year now. Before I could see more, my father came in. I thought he was going to shout at me, I thought he would scold me. But he only asked me to leave. The door has been locked again.

I wish I knew what my father is thinking. I don't mind if he is not thinking of me, I just want to know. What does he wake up and think of? Does he miss sleeping in the same bed as my mother?

My dad thinks the hospital will change everything for us. That it will just take a little more time, a little more money, a little more patience and the hospital will make our lives. I haven't heard him say that in a while. Ali says he is fida over me. My father is fida over the hospital.

Chhoti Bibi didn't come back for a few days as I told you on the phone. She somehow got on a bus with my pink bicycle and went to her cousin's house in Lyari, one of those neighbourhoods always in the papers because of a riot or a murder or several. She won't tell me her cousin's name or what she did there. She just shakes her head with a deep, knowing smile on her face.

She and Bibi act as if nothing has happened which I take to be the result of living with my family. Haha.

I almost got into an argument with my mother about it. I asked her if we should be worried about what had happened to Chhoti Bibi while she was gone. She had been gone for four days and three nights. My mother looked at me blankly.

I thought, how callous. Surely my mother has a responsibility towards a seventeen-year-old girl living in her house. Anything could have happened to Chhoti Bibi. Then I saw that she had been crying. The skin beneath her eyes had turned grey and wrinkled like a dead rat that had washed up into our garden last monsoon.

My mother saw me looking and she lifted a hand to her cheek and rubbed at where the tears had tracked. 'Your father didn't come home last night,' she said.

'He was at the hospital.'

She gave a short bark of a laugh I haven't heard before and went into the bathroom. The tap ran for a long time before I heard her splash water on her face.

My father was at the hospital. Truly. I'm absolutely certain he is not having an affair. I know this because I followed him a few months ago. He just goes to the hospital and stays there all day long. There are no women in the hospital except the nurses and they are all married and mostly old and fat.

My mother came out and sat down at her dressing table and began to comb her hair. It fell around her in soft glossy curls even though I could tell she hadn't washed it in days.

'He was at the hospital,' I said again. 'I'm sure he was at the hospital.'

She looked at me at the mirror and smiled. 'Tell me about Chhoti Bibi,' she said. 'Why were you so worried? What happened?'

I told her what happened and she frowned. Then she called Bibi and scolded her for not letting her know that Chhoti Bibi had come back.

So you see, my mother had known about Chhoti Bibi all along. She hadn't forgotten, hadn't disappeared. I shouldn't have doubted her. I should be a better daughter.

My mother came out of her room yesterday. We had tea together in the evening and Bibi made samosas in honour of the occasion. Even Navi was there by some miracle although he came late and was sweaty and rude and said the samosas were burnt when really, they were just crisp. She asked him questions about school but he gave one-word answers. He can be such a brat. I told her all about my college applications and she agreed with all my choices. Which is no small thing, Tania, because you know, my mother was admitted to all the colleges she had applied to, including Harvard and Yale. I have no idea why she went to Wellesley.

My mother sat on the verandah and had tea with us. She talked to me about school and laughed at an excellent joke I made. We sat there for a long time, the three of us, drinking several cups of tea and even though I really needed to use the bathroom, I didn't get up until it got dark and my mother went inside. I sat by myself in the garden with the flies and the invisible birds and wished that every day would end like this, with my mother and my brother sitting beside me eating burnt samosas.

Love,
Tanya

~

*March 14, 1992*
*Bombay*

Dear Tanya,

Something bad happened at school today and I was a part of it. I don't know how to tell Nusrat. She's going to hate me.

I came home in a bad mood but it didn't help that my parents were arguing at the dinner table. Of course.

'How can you blindly follow the Congress after all these years?'

'What is the alternative? A goonda gang of thugs?'

'That is so unfair! You're not even giving them a chance!'

My mom started shrieking. 'So they will destroy a mosque? Destroy our culture, destroy our country?' A piece of spinach flew out of her mouth and landed in the daal.

'Mom, can I have the vegetables?'

'You're the only businessman—sorry, businessWOMAN I know who doesn't support the BJP Sraboni. Your hypocrisy is unbelievable! Do you remember when our country went BANKRUPT?'

'Please Shayon, don't even pretend to know about the economy, you'll just embarrass yourself.'

'Mom, can I have the vegetables?'

'What you really mean is I'll embarrass you, don't you? Say it, for once just say it! Let's stop this pretence.'

'Say what Shayon? I'm tired. I worked really late today.'

'Say it Sraboni! Just SAY IT!'

'GIVE ME THE FUCKING VEGETABLES MOM!'

I hadn't meant to but somehow I was standing up with a glass of water and my empty plate in my hand. My mom was staring at me, her mouth open and full of food. My dad was pushing his chair back from the table and I was so scared he was going to leave, so scared that it would be another night of their fighting. The glass slipped out of my hand and fell to the floor and smashed.

'What's WRONG with you Tania!'

I started screaming. Everything! Everything was wrong! How could they not see it? How could they be so blind? Fighting about stupid things that don't matter when someone's life was destroyed in school today. Stupid BJP, stupid Congress, my parents should have them for children.

Of course it was my father that came to my room with a plate of food. He knocked on the door and peeped in with a big smile as if I was five years old. I wasn't hungry anymore but I let him sit down next to me. He stroked my hair and I let him.

'Why are boys so mean? Are men mean like that?'

'Was someone mean to you?'

I began to tell him what had happened. Even though I knew he wouldn't like it. Even though I knew his smile would disappear and he would begin to fidget and look anywhere but at me, I began to tell him.

I had always hated Aniket. Bopping around with his falling-off pants, thinking he is a hip-hop millionaire instead of a wannabe, gonnabe diamond merchant whose parents grew up in the village, pissing in the field. A loser who can't play any sports and only stopped wetting his bed last year. Do you think no one knows? Just because you threw a new year's party, you think people don't laugh at you behind your back? Everyone knows, Aniket, everyone KNOWS.

But I had never thought he would stoop as low as he did today.

He humiliated her. He made her into an outcast.

His girlfriend. Samara. They had sex last weekend. They have been together for two years now.

We were sitting around in the Assembly Hall at lunchtime like we always do. Aniket came in with a lassi moustache and Nishant made fun of him and Aniket said something mean about Nishant's parents not being rich and Nishant said that he'd rather have poor parents than parents who have to pay lakhs of rupees to keep their son in school.

And in like a weird coincidence everyone else stopped talking just then so everyone heard Nishant. People laughed. Samara laughed.

She should have known better. I had a bad feeling about it from the start.

Aniket asked her to go to the auditorium with him which is where people go to make out. And she said no. And again everyone heard.

Aniket's face was sweaty and scrunched up like he needed to go to the bathroom. But he was looking at her like a Hindi movie villain. And he said, 'That's not what you said on Sunday.'

Samara said loudly, 'NO ANIKET!'

That was a dumb thing to say. She's so dumb, honestly.

Aniket said again, looking around slowly at all the faces looking at him. He said, 'That's not what you said on Sunday when you were naked on my bed and I was fucking you so hard you cried.'

Everyone heard that. Aniket knew everyone was going to hear that.

He jumped up on the steps and shouted, 'She was NAKED! She was naked like a baby! She was high as a kite! Drug addict bitch in my bed!'

Who gave her the coke Aniket? Who took off her clothes?

He made it sound cheap. He made her sound cheap. How is it that the boys always get to decide? Arjun decides when we can tell people about our relationship. Aniket decides when to tell people that he fucked his girlfriend. And when did it become that? When they had sex, Samara said he had called it making love.

And she just sat there, on the floor, looking at him stupidly, blinking, blinking, not saying anything, not doing anything, just blinking and blinking.

And everyone got up and walked away from her, one by one, as if she was garbage, as if just moments ago, Gita hadn't sat with her arm around Samara. It was like Samara had sex and that was a cut-off point. Now she is no longer Gita's best friend. As if they hadn't been best friends since nursery school. As if nothing mattered except that Samara had had sex with the wrong person.

As if Samara had sex on her own.

My father got up. 'I'll get your mother.'

I knew he was going to say that. I also knew that he understood but he didn't think it was right for him to understand. My dad has weird ideas about this stuff. I didn't want my mother. She would tell me to stop wasting my time with people who are not 'serious'. That my problem is that I don't have any 'serious' friends. She wouldn't like Samara. Samara should have been writing college essays instead of having sex.

After Lunch, no one sat next to Samara. She sat alone. She was so pale and the tears kept coming even though she had a handkerchief propped up right below her eyes to catch them. She looked so beautiful and so sad. She reminded me of a goddess, sitting there all tall and beautiful and pale except she looked so sad and everyone around her thought the worst things. Already the notes had gone around, already ugly cartoons were in pockets.

I felt a hand on my head. It wasn't my mother. It was Nusrat! She had stayed behind for me. She came and sat next to me and put her beautiful arms around me. I felt her, I smelt her. I started crying. She understood like she always does. She tucked my head against her throat and wrapped her arms tightly against me. I love how Nusrat smells. Lyril soap and detergent and something else without a name. She understood without my saying anything. She always understands. I cried and cried and cried until there were no tears left and my head hurt.

I had stopped no one from leaving at Lunch. I had said nothing. Everything I wanted to say and do was drowned under relief that it hadn't been me, that it hadn't been Arjun, that I was not Samara, that I was not sitting in class, beautiful, tall and alone.

I asked Nusrat if she was ashamed of me and she didn't say anything. She would have stood up for Samara. She defends people. She takes care of people.

Halfway through the class after Lunch, Samara couldn't take it anymore. She began to put her books in her bag, crying loudly. The teacher didn't know what to do. He just stood there, twisting the chalk round and round in his hands until everything was white, including where he touched his brown pants. But no one laughed. We watched Samara leave, crying, her bag open and a book almost falling out of it.

I felt so bad for her but I also felt so glad that it wasn't me. So glad.

I told Nusrat that. She held my hand tightly.

The thing is, Tanya, if I'm so glad it wasn't me, how come it feels like it was?

Love,
Tania

~

*March 23, 1992*
*Karachi*

Dear Tania,

Chhoti Bibi was really upset with your letter. She thinks you should have marched up and reported everyone to the teachers including Samara because of course she also thinks it's awful that she had sex before marriage. She kept saying it over and over again until I got really irritated and told her that school teachers are not like the police to whom you go report crimes so they fix everything. She looked at me and said very seriously, 'Of course not Baji, teachers are actually good people, right?'

I am less surprised that you didn't say anything. I've always thought it must be hard to be popular. I stay clear of such things. Keep your head down and focus on the work, my dad had told me once when I was nine years old and hadn't been invited to a birthday party.

I have some good news. Some really good news. I'm actually very excited but I don't want to come across as insensitive but really, it is very good news.

First, I got Head Girl. I mean it was a foregone conclusion for the most part. I have been told I'm going to get Head Girl ever since Class Five. The only thing missing from my portfolio in Middle School had been sports and I've cultivated that in

Senior School. No one is surprised. But it feels great. Perhaps my father will want to take us all out to dinner?

The other really good news is that Chhoti Bibi has agreed to take a correspondence course with an NGO that provides remedial support to students to get their school leaving certificate. Although her English is still terribly weak, I have some hopes for the other subjects. She's allowed to fail one you know.

My friends are happy for me about making Head Girl. Perhaps if they had been surprised, there would have a party or a dinner or something. But everyone expected it. No one throws parties when you are expected to get it.

My pre-applications are all here and so are Ali's. I sent for his because he would have never remembered them on his own. The Harvard brochure is breathtakingly beautiful.

Are you going to throw a tantrum if I ask you if you have received your pre-applications?

Love,
Tanya

~

*April 1, 1992*
*Bombay*

Dear Tanya,

You get mad at your family for not talking about stuff but it's not like you're different. Every time I send you a letter that has hard stuff in it, you ignore it.

Things are still pretty bad for Samara, thanks for asking. But at least I talk to her. None of the other girls talk to her. And there are only twelve of us in the Commerce section, the rest are all boys. And before you ask, no I did not want to study Commerce, my mom made me. It was either Commerce or Science and I didn't have the grades for Science.

So far I haven't lost popularity because I talk to Samara. I try to keep it random you know. Like some days I'll be totally pally with her and other days I ignore her. It's better to make people wonder what you think of them rather than wonder what they think of you.

I'm worried about Arjun. He's been really moody and sad lately. I guess I may as well tell you he was suspended again and this time for two weeks. This is a super big deal because he is going to miss the monthly exam which will totally screw up his grades. I mean I don't care because we have decided we're not going abroad to college but his dad gets really mad and then he hits him with a belt. And when his dad gets mad Arjun goes batshit crazy. That's when he gets mean with me. It's his dad's fault really, not Arjun's.

I talked to Nusrat about it but I don't know, ever since the Samara thing she's been really touchy with me. She told me to not talk with Arjun anymore and like I called him the next day and she got so mad. She actually threw down the saucepan she was cleaning when I told her. I was kind of pissed off. I mean she's being paid to wash it not break it. I didn't say anything but I don't think it was cool.

What's the big deal? Why is she so mad? This has happened a gazillion times.

With all of this stuff going on, I totally ignored the stupid packages from American colleges that my mom had sent for. There's a whole pile in the corner of my room that she dumps a new one on every day. I swear there are fifty applications there.

So today she flipped her lid because I spilled coffee and some of it got on the application for Smith which is her second choice. What's the big deal, we can send for another one and anyway I'm not going. I just have to tell her that.

So basically everyone is mad at me and I'm working super hard at school and am really tired so please write back something normal without going on and on about college. Tell me about your brother. You like never talk about him.

Love,
T

~

*April 10, 1992*
*Karachi*

Dear Tania,

How can we be the same age and have such different problems? Your boyfriend got suspended, my boyfriend may get kidnapped. You are worried about some stupid fight at school and how that's going to decrease your social cache, I'm worried about whether either of my parents remembered to pay our school fees. You're angry with your mother for caring so much about where you go to college and my mother is barely aware that I'm alive. Is she even alive?

She has gone back to her room, Tania. I don't know what happened. Everything was going so well. For a whole week. She was getting up in the morning and coming out of her room to say bye to us before school. I dropped all my extra classes to come straight home from school and every time I entered the house, I'd be terrified that she'd be back in her room but no, every day, this last week, she was sitting downstairs in the living room, reading or taking a nap or once, mending the hem of my school uniform. I thought things were getting better.

Stop asking me about my brother because I know almost nothing about him. It's like he isn't there. He and my father float in a pool of nothingness in perfect harmony. I don't know what he does, I don't know what he's like, he's secretive and strange and the only time I know he's in the house is when he's locked up in the bathroom using up all the hot water. I used to wish we went to the same school but now I'm glad we don't because I can't tell what would be worse—to see him laugh and talk with other people or to see him not. I don't know my brother so stop asking.

But everything was getting better. My mother had come out of her room and now she has gone back in. I went and knocked on her door but it was locked and she didn't open it. I don't know what she is doing in there. I am scared that she is not doing anything in there.

Things are also really bad outside. I don't understand this country. We had to leave school early three times this week because of riots and yet, there is no report of that on the news. Things happen, we all leave the school in panic, and then there's no report of anything which leaves you wondering if you had imagined all of it. Had we imagined the kidnapping threats, the boys missing from school, the boys being sent away to boarding schools in America and England and Australia? Are we imagining the news of dead men turning up in ditches without eyes and fingers and noses? Are we imagining the strikes that send us scurrying home in the middle of a history test (that I would have topped if only we could have completed it)?

Am I imagining that my mother ever came out?

Nothing makes sense anymore. There's a line in a poem by William Butler Yeats that I learned by heart over the weekend and it keeps going round and round in my head—the centre cannot hold. The centre cannot hold, the centre cannot hold.

I just need it to hold until I go to Harvard. One more year.

Love,
Tanya

# 6

April 19, 1996
New York, NY

Dear Tania,

You had asked me about my brother and I never told you anything about him. This is my brother.

He got into Cal Tech the day I didn't get into Harvard. Had I ever mentioned that my brother is smarter than I am? The reason he didn't go to my school is that he got a scholarship for the American School. We had both applied for it when we were ten years old. He got it.

My brother chose not to go to Cal Tech. I don't know how it came to be that we chose sides with my parents. But it was always there from as long as I can remember. Navi somehow understood my father and my father somehow tolerated Navi. Much better than he tolerated me. Maybe it's because Navi wanted to be a doctor from when he was six years old. Or maybe Navi wanted to be a doctor because of my father. It's entangled.

When things broke, my brother and I cleaved the way we had grown up. My mother and I came to America and Navi stayed with my father in Pakistan. He is at Agha Khan studying medicine. I've *always wanted to ask him why he applied to Cal Tech at all. He came to visit over the summer and he spent a couple of weeks with me here at Columbia. I was working as a research assistant to a celebrity Law professor, Austin Weatherford. He's a terrible person but it will look really good on my CV.*

*Navi has grown up to be quite good looking. I remember you always used to think he was good looking. I had been quite nervous about his visit. Actually I had a panic attack about it and had to get on anti-anxiety medication. But it ended up being quite alright. I felt terribly awkward in the beginning but he seemed genuinely happy to see me. He really liked the campus and came with two tennis rackets. We used to play tennis together when we were children. Actually we played all the way until the summer before the year I broke my leg. It's the one thing we kept from our twin childhood in America. He was very impressed with the facilities at Columbia and amazed that we have so many tennis courts. He said there are no tennis courts at his college. I thought he was angry but then I saw that he had a big, satisfied smile on his face. He said, to no one in particular, 'My sister goes here for free.'*

*We didn't talk that much. We mostly played tennis and walked around the city. I had made plans to take him to all the museums and parks but he seemed uncomfortable and bored. So finally, we just walked around the city together all day, stopping for hot dogs and kebabs and slices of pizza.*

*He seems happy. He likes the work and wants to become an orthopedic surgeon. I didn't ask him why he doesn't want to become a neurosurgeon. I didn't ask him what our father thought about it. I didn't ask about my father.*

*When Navi was leaving, he gave me a hug and asked me to call home once in a while. I couldn't tell whether he meant call him or call my father. I haven't but Navi and I write emails to each other sometimes. His are short and mostly filled with descriptions of surgeries he has watched and trips he wants to take. I take hours to make mine the right length. First I write out everything I want, including the crazy stuff and the angry stuff and then I count the number of words in his email and pare mine down to within 15% of his. It's always 15% more.*

*For a long time, I was angry with Navi for never asking me what happened. Chhoti Bibi told me he stayed with me the whole time I was at the hospital for mad people. Slept on a bed he insisted they put in my room. I have no memory of this.*

*But how can a scientist have so little curiosity? He has never brought it up with me afterwards. He never asked my mother why she left either. Never asked her when she was coming back. Never asked her to stay. It used to drive me mad.*

*But I don't mind it now. It's kind of nice actually. Navi eschews complexity but that also means he is never exhausting.*

*I haven't had a bad dream in nine days. This is the first time since it happened that I've gone a whole week without waking up in the middle of the night. I am almost scared that it has happened. My therapist told me it would, I have been hoping and praying that it would. I started writing you these letters in the hope that it would. But now that it has happened I'm scared. I don't want to forget. I don't want to stop writing to you. I don't want to stop apologizing. I never want to stop feeling sorry, I never want to stop feeling sad because I don't know how to live without it anymore.*

*I will not stop writing to you Tania. I will never stop writing to you.*

*Love,*
*Tanya*

~

*April 20, 1992*
*Bombay*

Dear Tanya,

Today I won five prizes in school including Esprit de Corps which sounds like a perfume but means that I have team spirit. No one else got five prizes among the girls. Shondip got seven prizes but there are many more prizes for boys than for girls.

My mom didn't come to the ceremony because she is in Bangalore for a work meeting. My dad is angry about it. He says he is angry that she is not there for me but I think he just feels insecure because he never gets to travel for work. My mom travels business class and has an office car and driver.

I think my mother needs to watch it. She comes home from work really late and she looks tired and her sari is rumpled. My mother's sari was never rumpled before she started work. I can't remember the last time she cooked for us. These days it's always the cook. I mean she cooks better than my mom so I don't really mind but I know my dad does.

If I were my dad I would like totally have an affair. Arjun's dad is having an affair and my dad is much, much better looking. Also my dad is nice.

I'm totally not going to be like my mom. I'm always going to look hot for Arjun. But I'm not going to wear saris when I grow up, did I tell you that? Arjun is so cute he's like no T you gotta wear saris so I can think of your white, white stomach during my work meetings and get hard. I was like what do I think of during my work meetings and he's like you're not going to work.

He's joking. Relax.

Nusrat was really happy about my prizes. I got three cups and two medals. She wanted to polish the cups but I told her there's no point because I only get to keep it for a few days and then I have to give it back.

Nusrat doesn't have any cups even though she comes first like every year except in Class 3 when she was sick. She's still pretty upset about that. She brought all her certificates to show me and they're like neatly wrapped in plastic in this old Amarsons bag and then wrapped in brown string. That brown string killed me. Where do you even buy brown string? I'm pretty sure they don't have it at the shops I go to. But Nusrat has totally different stuff than I do. Her pens and pencils are different. Her underwear is different. She loves scotch tape, did I tell you that? She like goes CRAZY for scotch tape.

Anyway so I saw all her certificates. Nusrat Mohammedbhai first in Class 1, first in Class 2, first in Class 4, first in Class 5. Nusrat Mihammedbhai, first in English. First in everything. Then I saw a certificate that she had drawn up herself and coloured in with black felt pens to look like the other ones. It said Nusrat Mohammedbhai, first in Class 3. I acted like it was totally normal so I don't think she realizes that it's super weird.

I still haven't told my mom that I don't want to go to college in America. My dad knows. I mean I didn't even have to tell him. But he says I have to tell my mom, he's not going to tell her for me.

I wish he would but my dad is not brave and it's probably not a good idea anyway. At least I win some of my fights with my mother, my dad doesn't even really try. He always gives up halfway.

I can't leave my life here, Tanya. Today I went to Xavier's with a friend who goes there now. I really liked it. It's beautiful and there are lots of good-looking kids there. I don't want to leave Nusrat and my house and my room and go anywhere. I don't understand why my mom wants me to go so badly. You'd think she'd want to save her money and have at least one kid at home right?

You think that she's maybe thinking that once both Sammy and me are out of the house, she's going to divorce my dad?

I need to tell her that I'm not going to go to college in America. Tell me how to tell her. Do you think your mother could talk to my mother?

Love,
T

~

*April 28, 1992*
*Karachi*

Dear Tania,

Remember how you told me that I ignore your hard letters? Well, I just wanted to say, in the spirit of being factual: you do too. You haven't asked about my mother. You haven't asked if there have been any more kidnapping threats. And you haven't congratulated me about becoming Head Girl.

On that note, let me start by congratulating you on your prizes. Were all of them for sports? I don't think Esprit de Corps sounds like a perfume. Perhaps you should consider taking up French.

I just don't understand why you don't want to go to college in America. Don't you want a better life? And if that was a joke about my mother speaking to your mother, it wasn't funny.

I am thinking through my summer plans. Remember my to-do list from when my leg broke? I've completed most of the items on it except Chhoti Bibi. I had really hoped that she would be further along by now than she is.

I don't know what to do with her. It's not that she's not clever, she is. She gets concepts quickly and I really think she will do well in Science. But I just can't get her to do Math or to study the social sciences. And she is only allowed to fail one subject to pass the whole exam. I don't understand why she won't just sit down and learn History and Geography. It's the easiest because it doesn't require any thinking. How many centimetres of rain does it take for a successful cotton crop? 400cm. Which year was the first battle of Panipat? 1526. It's all in the book. I don't understand why she won't do it.

She has become quite stubborn as well. Earlier all I had to do was ask her to learn a page by heart and she would do it then and there, sitting right in front of me. Now she argues with me about why she needs to know when Babar lost Samarkand and what does that have to do with Pakistan anyway. The other day she argued with me for a full hour until finally I had to bribe her with an episode of 90210—with the AC on—before she agreed to learn by heart the chapter on weather patterns in Punjab. And it's the smallest chapter.

It can't go on like this. I am losing all power and authority. I have to argue with her to spend time studying with me and bribe her to do her homework. The exam is only three months away and she is nowhere near prepared. And if she fails I can't put it in my college applications.

And yet, it is not only that.

It is like she has become a different person. I guess she has become used to my golden hair and light eyes. I am no longer her fairy doll. She no longer wants to hear the story of how my parents met. Had I told you about the time I had asked her to write out a page of English grammar ten times and she wrote it out a hundred times? When I asked her why she did that she said she had wanted to make me happy.

And now she stalks into my room late and doesn't even blink when I ask her why she hasn't done her homework. She has begun to harangue me to go out, to go to parties, to spend time with Ali, to not sit at my desk like a mole allergic to the sun, an expression I strongly suspect she has made up.

I want to blackmail her and say, Chhoti Bibi, it makes me sad when you don't do your homework. Don't you want to make me happy anymore? But I am scared she will look at me with her dead black coal eyes and say: No Baji. No.

And who am I without my light eyes and golden hair? A hiding, crouching kind of person.

Chhoti Bibi strode into the house on her first day here. I'll never forget that. Unlike Bibi in all her sourness and my mother in all her translucence, Chhoti Bibi makes you feel like the world is exactly as it should be.

That's what Nusrat sounds like to me as well. Isn't it funny Tania, how you and I are the ones born into privilege and yet it's these two who know exactly who they are and where they're going?

Except of course I know where I'm going. Harvard. Are you sure you want to stay exactly where you are?

Love,<br>
Tanya

~

*May 5, 1992*
*Bombay*

Dear Tanya,

You don't really think that I'm like you, do you? You're kidding right? I mean, like how could you?

I've decided to have sex with Arjun. I can't make him wait any longer and actually, I'm dying to have sex. We've come really close many times and really, last time…never mind. You won't understand.

Nusrat is really angry with me about this. Ever since I told her I had decided to have sex with Arjun she won't talk to me. She doesn't stay after finishing her work. She just leaves without telling me.

Do you think she's jealous? She doesn't have a boyfriend. She's actually kind of not really developed in that way. She's so small and slight and somehow I can't even imagine her with a boy. It makes me feel a bit sick.

Anyway, I've decided to take control of my life. I'm going to have sex with Arjun. I'm going to tell my mother that I'm not going to college in America.

I'll say, Mom, I have something I need to tell you. And then I will explain to her how college in India will be better for the career I want and that I'll work really hard at Xavier's and how lots of famous people went to Xavier's and how I can do internships while going to college so by the time I graduate I will already have so much work experience and will be way ahead of my class.

My dad said the most important thing to tell her is that I'm going to be happier here than there. I don't know. I think my mom is too practical for happiness. Sometimes my dad says stuff and I want to be like, dad do you know anything? He doesn't get real life. He thinks the world is a lot simpler than it is. Sometimes I'm glad he married my mom because she's a lot sharper about things and takes care of things. Then sometimes I'm not because she hurts him with the sharpness.

My parents are so different. Like at parties sometimes I watch him and he doesn't look like he's enjoying the party as much as she is. I think he's fine when there are a few people but not the big parties with lots of people and my mom always in the centre, always beautiful and surrounded, laughing with everyone. That's never my dad. I've seen him look at her when she's like that. And then when he leaves the room and walks outside to go to the balcony for a cigarette, I've seen her look at him.

Maybe if I can solve my parents' marriage, my mom will say I don't have to go to college in America. You think I should ask?

Love,
Tania

~

*May 15, 1992*
*Karachi*

Dear Tania,

No, I don't think you should ask. I don't think you can solve your parents' marriage. Your parents' marriage doesn't need solving.

Thank you for calling. I'm sorry I hadn't written in a while. I've been feeling a little out of it I suppose. Ali left for his summer in London and it's lonely without him. My friends are also all in London. Sometimes I wish my parents had sent me to another school where there were other families who don't spend the summer abroad.

You know, I feel less tense talking to you on the phone than writing to you. In letters, I feel like I have to come up with exciting things to say to keep your attention.

How did Nusrat feel about our conversation? I admit, I felt a little awkward. Could you tell? Did you notice how Chhoti Bibi kept interrupting me?

In your letters, your friendship with Nusrat is anomalous. It stands out from everything else about you. But on the phone it makes sense. It doesn't fit exactly but it doesn't seem as odd.

Although it is odd, of course. We're both odd to be friends with girls who are paid to clean our homes. It's very odd that the only girl my age I spend time with is the girl also scrubbing out my toilet. And that I spend so much time worrying about whether this girl will like my lesson plan for the day.

Forgive me for being a bit of a wet blanket. Summer oppresses me. It is searing hot outside and the sun is cruelly close. I've always hated summer every single year ever since we came back from America. For the first few years, we would go to America, my mother, Navi and I, and stay with my grandparents in Boston. We used to have bicycles at their house that we would ride around and every evening my mother would buy ice cream cones for all of us and we would sit on the porch and eat them. We used to spend the whole day at the community pool where I had lots of friends because everyone looked like me. Sometimes when I go to the pool at the club here, the smell of the chlorine brings back such an intense longing, I turn around and leave.

We haven't gone to America the last two summers. I'm not really sure why not. Somehow the tickets were never bought last year. This year I didn't even expect it.

You're going to think it's strange that I never asked why. Navi didn't either. But Navi has always fit better in Pakistan. Maybe it's because he looks Pakistani. But even if Navi was blonde and blue-eyed in sub Saharan Africa he would be fine. He would find a sport to play and be quite happy doing his own thing. That's what he says when I ask him what he's doing. My own thing.

I don't have a thing that's mine except school. It's worst in summer when it physically hurts to step outside. So here I am inside, in Chhoti Bibi's beloved AC, books open and computer on but somehow even here, the sun intrudes, even through shut windows and drawn curtains and there is nowhere further to retreat except perhaps into this self-pitying missive that I will end and seal into an envelope straight away so as to prevent myself from tearing it up and throwing it away.

Love,
Tanya

P.S. I woke up in the middle of the night and saw my mother outside in the garden. She was crawling around the jasmine plants. She was patting the soil into place and rubbing each leaf with a napkin. When I went down to get her, I saw that she was wet and shivering. She let me put my arm around her and take her back to her room. She was so thin, so small, I could have carried her. I don't want to talk about this, Tanya so please don't mention it in your reply. And please don't tell anyone. Not even Nusrat.

~

*May 24, 1992*
*Bombay*

Dear Tanya,
    Last night I had sex with Arjun and I'm still shivering.
    Okay, I've said it. Don't ask me any questions. I don't want to talk about it.
    That sucks man that you can't go to America for the summer holidays. Why didn't you even ask if you can go? I don't get it. Maybe they like forgot. And just because you didn't ask you don't get to go. I don't get it. You could have just asked.
    Fuck it. I have to talk about it.
    Every minute every breath every smell.
    I want to write it all and then learn it by heart and say it like a poem before going to sleep at night without him.

Without him. I can't live my life without him. It hurts so much.

I mean not there though that hurt a LOT which no one tells you and I am going to tell everyone. But I mean how much it just hurts the whole thing but it's like it is not of this world or this life. Like I've never believed in heaven or hell and then this happens and you feel like someone has opened a curtain and you realise it's not about heaven or hell, it's about this world and how much there can be in it.

I can't stop shivering.

It was at the Taj. He had always told me it would be at the Taj because it's the best hotel in the city and also because it's the only hotel where he knows someone who knows someone who wouldn't check ID.

It was in the evening right after sunset. I felt damn nervous even though I was wearing my lucky bra and my hot boots. We kind of just stood there looking at each other and we both sort of giggled. Then he came close to me and touched my arm just my arm and his hand was shaking. He looked at me and there was no one no one in the whole world who has wanted me so much who has loved me so much except maybe my dad. And I remember being grossed out by thinking that and then he pulled me close and held me and he was shaking. Arjun was shaking. I started crying.

It happened very slowly. He switched off the light and I wanted to say no because I wanted to see everything but I had forgotten how to talk and I could do nothing except look at him looking at me. He tried to close the curtain but it was a mechanical curtain and he didn't know how.

I thought he'd have moves you know. I thought he'd pick me up and take me to the bed and I thought that it would be passionate and wild. But in the end, I held his hand and walked to the bed and he just followed me.

He told me later that he had meant to have music. He had a whole cassette of songs that he had like prepared specially for this. But he forgot to put it on.

You know how in the movies the clothes come off so perfectly and everything is just passion passion passion? It wasn't like that. It took ages and things got stuck. But when I saw his chest and his arms and I knew he had worked out that morning because of the veins that were popping near his wrists just how I like it I began to cry again because it was so beautiful and he was so beautiful and the way he looked at me the way he touched me it was as if everything was for the first time. (Even though it was actually the ninth time he was seeing me naked.)

I had shaved down there because I was too scared to wax and there was a nick and it hurt when he touched it and he freaked out and said that if that was going to hurt then how were we going to have sex and then I told him it was the nick and he was so sweet he bent down and kissed it and kissed it and licked it and I thought my heart had stopped beating, it got so strange and I couldn't breathe and it seemed to go on forever and I focused on the lamp in the corner of the room which was green and had orange tassels all around the rim and I think maybe I had an orgasm.

He really liked that and then it got hard as in painful because he was pushing and I got really scared because it was still just with his hands.

He took his hand away and then I let him take off his shorts which I never had before and it looked so weird and so beautiful and he got upset when I said that because he said dicks aren't meant to be beautiful so I didn't say it again but it was beautiful and I wanted to touch it and hold it and never let it go.

Then he took out the condoms but his hands were shaking so it took a long time to open it. I wanted to open it for him because it was all going away but I wanted to be feminine and sexy so I just lay there and did nothing. He tore the first one and the second one snapped on his penis which really hurt so for some time we just lay there holding each other and that was really soft and I felt like my heart would burst the way he started touching me and the way his body felt under my hands as if it was water. He has no hair anywhere which makes me want to hold him like a baby.

And then he began to put it inside and it wasn't at all easy and we were like totally surprised because every time we've fooled around it just got to that point so quickly and both of us dying to do more and yet this time with everything in place with the condom with the hotel with the sea outside and the green lamp but it wasn't going in.

We stayed like that for a long time with him on top of me and we just kept kissing and kissing and kissing and his hands were in my hair just like how I like it and I was holding him close on top of me and I felt like the world would end if he moved even just a little bit and then slowly slowly it was like really painful he went inside and then once he was inside totally inside it was the best feeling I've ever had in my whole life and that was the point when it felt like I was seeing something I had never ever seen before even though the whole time I was really just looking at the green lamp with the orange tassels.

He came and his hands were so tight on my breasts that they hurt now. His face looked frightening like a mad person his eyes weren't blinking and he was sweating even though it was so cold in that room.

And then afterwards he just held me and shivered and I held him and shivered and we were both crying and saying I love you I love you I love you. I knew then that we were born to have sex because it is the best feeling of anything in the whole world to be joined like that with someone. I was born to have sex with Arjun.

His muscles kept quivering and it wouldn't stop being hard but it hurt too much so we didn't do it again and he whispered in my ear that he didn't even want to, he just wanted to lie there with me forever. Which is what I always want with Arjun but he has never wanted that with me.

The funny thing is I understand now why Nusrat didn't want me to do this. I am a different person. I loved Arjun before but now I belong to him. I know him like no one else knows him and he knows me like no one else knows me. Nothing compares to this kind of love.

I am shivering. It hurts everywhere and I think I have fever. I love him so much I almost want to die right now so I never have to feel anything else.

Don't say anything. Just please don't say anything.

Love,
Tania (lover of Arjun)

## 7

April 26, 1996
New York, NY

Dear Tania,

    You know what I like to do in New York when I feel sad? I like
to watch nannies in the park.

    New York is full of nannies. They are dark black, light black, milk
black, hazelnut black, almond black. The children are blue eyed, green
eyed, light brown eyed, strawberry blonde, golden blonde, chestnut
blonde, ginger. They wear polka-dotted tights with boots. They wear
darling little fur and leather jackets with matching hats and gloves.

    I watch the nannies wheel the babies up and down Park and
Fifth, Central Park West, Central Park South, Columbus and
Amsterdam. They pick them up and croon to them. The babies sigh
and tuck their heads into their shoulders, their miniature porcelain
hands curled tightly around dark, ungloved fingers.

    The older children play on the swings in the park. The nannies sit
on the periphery watching them. Sometimes they talk to each other
but not often. You can always tell the mothers from the nannies. The
mothers are young and dressed in designer sweatpants. The mothers
wear knee-length leather boots with double wool peacoats and soft
pastel cashmere scarves. The mothers grow smaller every time I see them.

*The nannies are large. They're usually in white Keds. Sometimes they wear uniforms. They wear polyester puffy jackets with red and white striped fleece scarves. They wear tight jeans with many pockets. They wear thick gold earrings that the babies like to pull at.*

*The nannies are usually from the Caribbean. Some are from Mexico and Guatemala and Peru. The ones from Jamaica and Trinidad are paid more because they speak English. The ones from Haiti are paid the least because their French is Creole.*

*The nannies leave behind families and children of their own to come here and work. Many of them come here illegally and they can't go back for years and years and years. They watch their own children grow up through photographs. They bring up other children here, one after another.*

*Many of my friends at Columbia have been brought up by nannies. Some talk about them like a loved but second-tier aunt. Others screw up their faces and try to remember names. She used to make an excellent pear tart, they'll say, in an effort to be helpful. She used to smell of cinnamon.*

*You never asked me why I did it, Tania.*

*Do you know how I used to wait for your letters? In the muddy, darkening swirl of days that was my last year in Pakistan, your letters were a talisman against the dark. Your letters made me feel normal. And yet, it began to be that when I had the envelope in my hand with its red and white borders and Mahatma Gandhi stamps, I would not want to open them. Her name crowded every page.*

*Nusrat, Nusrat, Nusrat.*

*Now I read your letters I can see that it's not true. But my mind was not normal then, Tania. You know that. You knew that then, didn't you? My mother scrabbling in the dirt, my father absent, just absent and Navi retreated into an inner world. And I, I was left. No one worrying about me. No one thinking of me first. No one putting me first. No one just for me.*

*I wanted you just for me.*

*I used to count the number of times you mentioned her in your letters. Five, seven, ten. Nusrat this and Nusrat that. I gloated when you didn't tell her things that you told me. I burned to show you my school certificates when you described hers.*

*It never made sense to me. She seemed so vastly good, so outside the sphere of you.*

*If you had asked me then why I did it I would have said, I wanted to be your best friend. If you ask me now why I did it, I would say the same thing except perhaps in more abstract words. Grown-up words. I would talk about primacy. I would talk about belonging and ownership. I would talk about bond creation.*

*I wanted to matter. That's all Tania. I thought that with you at least, I should matter first, matter more than a servant girl.*

*But that was all. It's pathetic that there isn't a deeper reason but there isn't. All I ever wanted was to come first. Everything else was a mistake, a circumstance that I could never have dreamt because who has that kind of black magic, who can conjure up what happened, that collective death of sanity?*

*You were my best friend, you know. The best friend I've ever had. Ever will.*

*Sometimes I feel like you think I should have been wiser, I should have been older. I could say the same to you. You mattered and you knew it. You could have taken better care of me.*

*Nannies matter and then they don't. They float from one family to the next. And yet, you see them in the park and they look so much in love. They watch the babies learn to walk with wonder in their eyes. They love and they leave and they love and they leave.*

*Nannies give me hope.*

Love,
Tanya

~

*June 6, 1992*
*Bombay*

Dear Tanya,

Dude, did you get my letter? How come you haven't responded?

I haven't told Nusrat. I haven't told anyone but I feel like it's written all over me that I did it.

I wonder if he feels that way. He has been really busy.

But that night, you know, afterwards, we came home and he called me and we talked forever in the dark, in whispers. And he kept telling me that he loved me and that he wanted to be with me forever. I think that's now my favourite memory. Lying there in my bed, things hurting down there and Arjun's voice on the phone, sounding like a little boy.

Before this, my favourite memory was of being six years old and jumping up and down on my bed right before my birthday party. I remember going up and up, being able to see the tops of buildings, my dress going up and down against my body, silk and air, silk and air.

Things were a lot simpler then, no? Birthday parties were about cake and presents. Boys were just people in shorts.

I guess the night with Arjun also felt like seeing the tops of buildings. Jumping higher, running faster than I ever have before. Silk and air. Except there was no silk, only cheap lace I bought from the street and it scratched everywhere.

Please write back man. I'm going crazy.

Love,
Tania

*June 16, 1992*
*Karachi*

Dear Tania,

I'm sorry I haven't written. I know you were waiting for me to respond.

I haven't written because I don't know what you want me to say. That I'm glad he was nice to you? That I was surprised he was nice to you? That I'm glad you used a condom? That I'm worried about what will happen now? Are you still not officially together in school?

I'm glad you haven't told Nusrat.

This morning I woke up early to go to the beach. I wanted to think through what I would write to you. Sometimes that can be really delicious you know. Thinking about what to say, what not to say. What to ask. What to hint at. What to leave out entirely.

When I went outside, I saw what I thought was a tablecloth that had fallen off the clothesline. It was my mother again. She was asleep this time. Bibi helped me bring her in, her lips pursed. She wouldn't look at me.

It happens almost every night now, Tania.

I hadn't meant to tell you this. I had meant to write only about you and what happened with Arjun. But look what happens when I pick up a pen to write you. Look what comes out.

The beach was quiet and empty because it was so early in the morning. You can see the fishermen's boats in the waves and if you looked really hard you could see their nets glimmering in the sun. Salman bhai, our driver, was nervous about me walking down the beach alone. He locked the car and walked behind me.

You want to know something funny? My memory of being six is Salman Bhai. We had just come to Pakistan from America and everything was new and difficult. I made Salman Bhai my best friend. I would talk to him for hours in the car, making up stories of tiny people in the vents of the car air conditioner. I would tell him about their lives, their families, their offices, their schools, their playgrounds, their meals, their beds, their chairs, their bathrooms. He always listened very seriously and asked me very good questions. He remembered their names and when one of them was bad and I would hit them, he would look at me reproachfully and say, Baba, why are you hitting such small people.

Now that I look back, I wonder if that had been my parents' plan, to just throw two six-year-olds into a completely new world in the hopes that we would swim. Well, they were half right.

But I hated everything. The sky which was yellow and not blue, the food which made my eyes water, the new people, the new school with the new language, everyone wearing different clothes and gates with barbed wire and the way all the girls looked at me, the new girl with doll hair and doll eyes. A new world where Navi left me.

I remember going to a birthday party where we were sent to play in the garden and the other girls decided that I was to be a traitor and hung from a tree. They found the hose from the garden shed and I started crying and Salman Bhai heard me and he came and picked me up. I remember being high up in his arms, the girls looking up at me with curiosity and disappointment. I wanted to stay in Salman Bhai's arms forever.

What is it about love? I went to the beach this weekend to feel closer to you, Tania, who I have never seen, living in Bombay on the other side of the sea, thinking of me only because I live here, far way and can't touch your perfect bubble life. That is why you haven't told Nusrat, right? Because she has the power to touch your bubble and change it. You only told me because I am far away, didn't you? Across the sea.

What is it about love? Behind me walked Salman Bhai. He walked several paces behind because that was his calculation to keep me safe while not upsetting me because I'm still Baji, I'm still the daughter of his employers. Salman Bhai knows where my friends live and who their parents are. Salman Bhai puts on loud music when Ali is in the car with me. Salman Bhai drives me home the long way in the monsoon so I can sit in the car by the sea and watch the rain fall. Maybe he likes it too.

You say that Arjun loves you. What do you mean by this love? Does he want desperately to be first in your life? Will he calculate to keep you safe? Would he count the days waiting for your letter?

What I decided to say to you this weekend on the beach is the distillation of what I have learnt: love is a suspicious thing. For every time it is blissful and sweet, there are seven times when it is absent. You won't listen to anything I say but be careful, Tania. Be careful.

Love,
Tanya

~

*June 26, 1992*
*Bombay*

Dear Tanya,

I need to talk to you. I'm writing this in school so Nusrat won't know. I'm going to post it on my way home so that you get it soon and can reply soon. I'm not allowed to call you anymore. Things are bad at home and somehow your mother keeps coming up but I'll go into that later.

The thing is Arjun is being a little weird. I mean not a lot, I'm probably overreacting. Just a little bit. For example, he hasn't called me since that night. I mean I've called him and he's taken my calls so it's not like we haven't talked at all.

I'm overreacting right?

And then last night we had just talked for seven and a half minutes and he said he had to go. He said he was going to go to Ashu's house to play video games.

But then today Ashu wasn't in school. He's not even in town.

The thing is Arjun lies all the time. Then he tells me about it and we laugh at how stupid people are for believing him. But he's never lied to me before.

I keep going over every single detail. He carried me to the lift and kissed me all the down to the lobby. We talked on the phone that night in whispers and it was all beautiful and perfect and he told me he was going to rent every hotel room for me so we could do it in a different room every night. Then he said he was going to pick me up for school the next morning which he has always refused to do before.

But the next morning he sent his driver. As if I don't have drivers.

It's nothing I can put my finger on. It's not like he's avoiding me or anything. We went to watch a movie. But he didn't try anything. And usually that's the only reason he wants to go to movies.

I'm imagining things right? That's why I am telling you all this. You're sensible and clever. You'll tell me that I'm totally overreacting and of course everything is fine. I mean we went to see a movie.

Please tell me that Tania. I have this sick feeling at the bottom of my stomach and it won't go away. I don't feel like going anywhere in case he calls. I have to pretend I'm okay and it's exhausting. I'm overreacting right? Nothing is the matter. He loves me.

Love,
Tania

~

*July 2, 1992*
*Karachi*

Dear Tania,

What do you mean my mother keeps coming up?

You're not overreacting. He's trying to break up with you. Did you get my last letter?

Love,
Tanya

~

*July 9, 1992*
*Bombay*

Dear Tanya,

I did get your last letter. I'm ignoring it because it was a bit weird.

But I like to go down to the sea too. This morning I took your letter and went down to the sea. The tide was in and the waves were monsters. I missed Nusrat. I miss Nusrat all the time. Is that weird?

Nusrat makes me feel like I used to feel when I was a kid and had a tent in my room and I used to go and hide there. Get into the tent and zip it up. And everything was okay.

It's become pretty tough to live with my parents these days except I can't tell if it's new or if I'm just like noticing it more. Do you ever feel like that?

I mean my parents have always argued and disagreed about most things. They'll sit down to have tea in the morning and my dad will pick up the newspaper and say something good about the BJP and everyone knows it's only to piss her off because he looks fake grave and sometimes even winks at me. But my mom will jump right in, before even her first sip of tea, breaking a biscuit into it and then forgetting all about it because it is just so important to make her point, to be right. Because, you know, she is always right. The biscuit never has a chance.

And then at some point it stops being funny and they're just mad at each other. And I'm always wondering how an argument about an election became 'you haven't forgiven me' and 'no, I will never forgive you'.

Yes, I did tell my mom about your mom. First of all, your mom is my mom's best friend. I think she's like her only real friend. I mean my mom has tons of friends but they're like matlabi friends. You do something for me I do something for you. And secondly, I'm like worried about your mom man. Not coming out of her room. That creeping around in the garden at night singing lullabies to flowers. Dude.

So basically I told my mom that your mom is in bad shape. I told her she's depressed. And for some reason that word really got my mom and she kept saying, depressed, depressed? Did Tanya say Lisa is depressed? How did she say it? In a serious way?

I was like no, she didn't use that word. And then my mom got mad at me and told me that I should know the meanings of words before using them.

Isn't depressed just a big word for sad?

It's not like my parents have been fighting about your mom. Exactly. I think my mom is worried about your mom. And I think my dad feels like my mom should be worried about him.

He doesn't say that but she applied for a visa to go visit your mom in Karachi without telling my dad and he's mad about that. He says that that's lying. He also thinks it's a bad idea for her to go to Karachi because of all the violence in Pakistan. He thinks that it's not safe and all that. And he says she's being irresponsible because of what would happen to us if anything happened to her.

And my mom got all bitter and was like, you're just worried about where the money will come from.

And my dad got silent like he does when my mom brings up money.

What I don't understand is that if my mom wanted to be with someone who would make a lot of money then why did she marry my dad? My dad's not ambitious. He's not one to charge ahead and stand up for things. My dad can't even decide what shoes to buy without my mom.

You're selfish for wanting to go to Pakistan when things are dangerous there.

No, you're selfish for not caring about Lisa. You've never cared about Lisa. You've never cared about anyone in my life, not my parents, not my sister, not my friends.

Your sister? What about the time when she was living in our house for nine months?

So what if she did? She's my sister. She can stay with us for nine years if she wants.

Yes, I'm sure you would have loved it if my parents had lived with us for nine years.

I TOLD YOU YOUR PARENTS CAN LIVE WITH US! I told you! You said you didn't want it!

You didn't really want them here, they could tell. You don't speak to them in Bangla.

I grew up in Bombay! How can I speak Bangla? And all the things I did for them, none of that matters right? Changing the toilet seat so it doesn't hurt Baba, getting soft mattresses, getting a second driver to come in the evenings for them, cooking mutton without garlic and onion….

Yes thank you Sraboni. Thank you for the supreme sacrifice of giving up onion and garlic in your mutton curry.

Oh please Shayon, you don't see the hypocrisy? Your parents are the only Brahmins who eat mutton without garlic and think they're saints.

Don't you dare call my parents hypocrites!

You're right, you're the real hypocrite. Forcing your son to do a racist, fascist ceremony.

I didn't force him to do the thread ceremony. Sammy wanted to do it.

He was ten! You bribed him with a new bicycle!

It went on for a while. I've personally heard them go round and round Sammy's thread ceremony at least twenty times.

Somehow it came back to your mom and my dad was screaming about how both my mom and I are more interested in what's happening in your house than in our house and how the last phone bill was insane and how he won't have it. So then it went back to money. And I went into my room and shut the door.

If money is so important to my mom how come she wants to spend loads of it to send me to college in America?

Arjun finally called yesterday. But then he said he had to go and he hung up in a few minutes. But if you're right and he wants to break up with me, how come he hasn't done it yet?

You know, my father is always the person to go after my mother to make up after a fight? Every time. I used to wonder that it doesn't make him feel bad but I think it actually makes him feel good. He'll go to her and she'll ignore him at first. And then he'll try to hug her from behind or hold her hand or something. And she'll still ignore him. And he's already looking happy you know, like a kid playing a video game he knows he's going to win. And slowly she'll start talking to him and he'll keep saying sorry sorry sorry and then finally her hand is in his hand and her fingers are holding his and my father looks like he has won a race.

They haven't made up yet from yesterday's fight. These days it takes them a lot longer to make up. What will happen if my dad stops going to my mom to make up?

I miss Nusrat.

Love,
Tania

~

*July 14, 1992*
*Karachi*

Dear Tania,

Why do you miss Nusrat? I know I should respond to your letter, especially about the fight at home but I can't. Not right now. Something bad has happened. My teacher's husband was shot. He's dead.

Mrs. Iqbal is our Chemistry teacher. She is also American. She is young and very thin. She wears long skirts with loose tops so that when she walks, the smallest breeze wraps her clothes all the way around her. Her collar bone is prominent, like a necklace she cannot take off. When she first moved to Karachi, my mother had invited her over for tea a couple of times.

We had Chemistry lab first thing this morning. We were studying the properties of hydrochloric acid today. What does it do to chalk. What happens when you add impurities. What happens when you crystallise it.

Mrs. Iqbal had written out the questions on the board and was sitting at her table watching us. Unlike other teachers, she never does other work in class with us, no correcting of papers, no filling out attendance registers. She just sits at her desk and watches us.

Rumour has it she was doing her PhD at the University of

Wisconsin at Madison in Theoretical Physics. Mr. Iqbal was doing a Master's degree in Political Science (on a full scholarship). They fell in love. He moved back to Pakistan and he convinced her to marry him and move back with him. She gave up her PhD, married him and moved to Karachi.

There must be something about Pakistani men, don't you think?

I was partnered with Sohail for the experiments. I was looking at the flame and thinking about how blue it was against the flash of its yellow heart when there was a thud. When I looked up, Mrs. Iqbal had fallen to the floor, her chair overturning behind her. Father Thomas, our Principal, had come in when I wasn't looking and was now standing next to her, looking down at her aghast.

Everyone looked at each other. Someone dropped a set of test tubes.

Father Thomas motioned to one of the boys and together they picked her up and carried her outside. I saw her face jerking over Imran's shoulder, her eyes wide open as if she recognized us and could do nothing about it.

When she left, the class descended into chaos. Someone said that Father Thomas had come in to tell Mrs. Iqbal that her husband had been killed on his way to the university where he taught Political Science. Later on I found out that he had been shot near the nallah right outside the road that leads to our school. He was shot seven times and his car drove into the water. I heard that his body was never found. I heard that the water stayed red for weeks.

But all I could think then, sitting in the old lab with newspaper-lined shelves of test tubes, is that maybe this is why my mother had gone silent. Maybe she has worried and worried about this moment happening to her and that one day the worry got too big, too heavy and she collapsed under it. Maybe that is what they talked about, my mother and Mrs. Iqbal when she had invited her over to tea. Maybe she had been warning Mrs. Iqbal that it was going to be like this.

The rest of the day passed in a daze. We had thought that we would be sent home but we weren't. The rumours began. He was with MQM and PPP did it. He was with PPP and MQM did it. He was a Baloch sympathizer and the government did it. He was a Kashmir sympathizer and the Indians did it. He was a spy and the Americans did it.

Throughout the day, I kept thinking about my mother. It had occurred to me that when she found out she would want to comfort Mrs. Iqbal. I imagined it over and over again. The phone ringing and someone telling her about it. Her hand going to her heart and tears coming to her eyes because a woman who cried over a dead plant would surely cry over a dead husband. I imagined her getting out of bed and phoning Mrs. Iqbal. I imagined her listening and making crooning voices on the phone and then going over to help Mrs. Iqbal pack to go back to America.

I almost ran home.

But when I got home, everything was exactly as I had left it. Bibi and Chhoti Bibi were in the kitchen. The door to my mother's room was closed. When I opened it, I could tell from the smell that she hadn't left it all day. She didn't say anything to me because she was crying, turned over on her side, her arms tucked deep into her chest. And I knew that she hadn't picked up the phone, hadn't left her bed, hadn't done anything else all day but cry at the red curtains she had made herself so many years ago when she had let me hem stiches into the lining and had laughed and laughed when I had stitched my dress into the curtain.

Mrs. Iqbal is not leaving. Pakistani men are persuasive. American women are foolish. But I, who come from both, am going to be neither.

Love,
Tanya

# 8

Dear Tania,

Can you believe that there are only two months left of college? Well, for me. Your college was three years, I know. You're in the real world already. What do you do now? Do you miss college? Did you make good friends there?

You would have loved the sports here at Columbia. I've enclosed some pictures with this letter. I just wanted you to see how pretty it is. Maybe you can send me some pictures of Xavier's? You don't even have to write me a letter. You could just send me the pictures.

I'm doing something quite peculiar. Well, peculiar for me. It's exactly what you would have done if you had come to college in America. Instead of going straight for my PhD, I've decided to postpone graduate school and go work in New York for a year.

I know. It's crazy.

My mother was surprised, I could tell. My professors are disappointed in me although they're all very polite here in America. Amrita asked me if I was sure. I almost said, no I've changed my mind, I'll apply for PhD programs in Political Science.

*But my therapist has been talking to me about this. She thinks I imagine that I'm letting people down. I don't know how she can think that I imagine it because I've told her everything. Every single detail, Tania, I swear. But she's American. They don't get these things.*

*I'm applying for jobs in New York. Investment banking jobs. Management consulting jobs. Their salaries sound like lottery tickets.*

*You used to get angry with me for being so desperate to come to college here in America. Do you know that by the time I left for college, we couldn't even afford to pay Salman Bhai or Bibi? They just stayed on. Salman Bhai is still with my father. I don't know where Bibi is. I think of her much, much more than I ever thought I would.*

*There were people in Karachi who loved me. Ali loved me. Salman Bhai loved me very much. Bibi loved me.*

*Except I can't tell if it is out of love or if it is out of allegiance. The odd thing is that Bibi lived with us in Karachi for nineteen years but her mind never left the village. And Chhoti Bibi lived with us for six months but she left the village the day she arrived.*

*Amrita would say that is ethnocentric of me. To posit urban mindsets as more progressive, as better. But the truth is that Chhoti Bibi overtook me in days. It shows even in my old letters to you.*

*You haven't asked about her. I thought you would have. She's fine. Or at least she was three and a half years ago when I left. She stayed with me through the whole time at the hospital for mad people. That was when she called you and you didn't pick up. I think she called you every day that I was there. You never picked up.*

*After that she came to visit me once before I left for college. She had found another job in a house with a child in it the age of her brother, Mohammad. I wonder what happened to him. I asked for her address to write to her and you know what she said to me? She said no. She said she doesn't want letters from me and she doesn't want to write me letters.*

*Isn't it odd how I'm the one who has always been unsentimental and cold and yet it is all of you, who say love in the first letter, who hug and kiss, who spent hours braiding my hair, who move on without looking behind? And here I sit, unmoved, unmovable me, holding onto old pictures, re-reading old letters, living in an imaginary world three and a half years later in which you pick up the phone when I call you and write back to my letters.*

*What are you doing now, Tania? Are you in an office somewhere, looking out at the rocks by the sea? What kind of work do you do? What do you wear to work, Tania? Do you wear saris like your mother? Don't you ever think about my mother, Tania? Don't you ever think about me?*

*Love,*
*Tanya*

July 24, 1992
Bombay

Dear Tanya,

Shit dude, that's insane. I'm so sorry. Nusrat and I are both so sorry.

Your reaction is a little weird. I mean your teacher's husband died and all you can think about is your mother.

Don't get mad at me but I told my mom about this. Not just because your mom's reaction is super weird and creepy but you too man. It's like you don't care about this teacher at all. Her husband died man.

I told Nusrat. About Arjun. I told her everything. I started crying. She just put her arms around me and held me. I cried for hours and hours. We were sitting on the rocks by the sea. At some point my head was in her lap and she was stroking my hair and kissing it. I closed my eyes and I could hear the waves and Nusrat's bangles against my hair. Her hand was so soft on my face. It's the first time I've felt like a full person since that night.

She wrote to me in her notebook, 'No matter what you do, I will always love you.'

Is that what you meant about love? That someone should love you all the time? Even when you've fucked up and feel like yesterday's spit on the ground.

My parents are still not talking to each other but they have both noticed that I'm sad. My mother asked me what's the matter and if it is to do with Arjun. I said no. My father never asks questions. He just hugs me. Once I was crying about something to my dad and when I looked up he was crying too. My mom is right. He is too soft.

Nusrat thinks I should break up with Arjun. But how can I break up with him when I don't want to?

Today Samara came and talked to me and was like crying and stuff because she wasn't invited to a party. I mean she's mostly fine now but still a few people act like she's a leper. I wanted to get angry but I felt so tired. So lethargic. Worrying about Arjun takes up all my time and energy.

Will I ever go back to being normal? I don't even want to go to the party. I don't know if Arjun will be there. It's like he has already broken up with me and has forgotten to tell me.

Love,
Tania

*August 2, 1992*
*Karachi*

Dear Tania,

I'm so sorry. I'm so sorry I couldn't even get my mother to come to the phone. I tried. I really tried. She wouldn't even look at me when I went to her room. I begged, Tania. I begged her to take your mother's call but she wouldn't get out of bed.

I finally managed to get Navi to talk about it. All he will say is that he doesn't know what to do and that it's not his fault. And that he has a squash match over the weekend.

How worried is your mother about my mother? Should I write to my grandparents in America? I've started letters to them but can't bring myself to finish one and send it. It feels disloyal.

It's 1 am at night and I'm waiting up for my father to come home. Things can't go on like this.

I'm so sorry. Please apologise to your mother. I did on the phone but please do it again.

Love,
Tanya

P.S. Your mother seems nice.

# 9

May 3, 1996
New York, NY

*Dear Tania,*

*I want to tell you the things I have been mad at you for. And I'm not doing this because my therapist thinks I should. I'm doing it because it's time you know. Neither one of us is perfect.*

*You shouldn't have loved Nusrat. You could have done all the things you did with her without that. This is your problem, you know Tania? This is your issue. Everything black and white, everything all or nothing. America is terrible, Bombay is everything. Your father good, your mother bad. School a victory or an indictment. It couldn't be enough for you to be friends with the girl who washed your dishes.*

*Oh you were such a cardboard stereotype. With your overbearing mother and your unfulfilled father. I don't believe they looked at each other at parties. I don't believe they held hands. I bet you made it up.*

*I'm mad at you for your holier-than-thou attitude. How many letters will it take? How many times have I tried to say I'm sorry? You know I am. I told you about the nightmares. I told you I can't have sex. I told you I can't sleep. I told you I've been going to a shrink for four years. I told you Chhoti Bibi left me. Do you think just because you were there it only happened to you? IT HAPPENED*

*TO ME TANIA. IT HAPPENED TO ME. If it happened to you
it happened to me.*

*You used me. For all your talk of popularity and being the queen
bee at school, you didn't have anyone to talk to either. You also came
home alone and ashamed because the only person you could talk to
was your servant.*

*You used Nusrat. If you hadn't pretended like Nusrat was your
best friend then none of this would have happened. But no, Tania
Ghosh doesn't see that her best friend is a servant, is Muslim, can't
speak, lives in a ghetto, has an illiterate father. Not Tania Ghosh. She
is above class. She is above religion. She is just so cute with her sassy
eyes and sassy tongue sashaying around with her servant best friend.*

*We all prepare and present a version of ourselves. I tried so hard
and always, always failed but you never even tried. Not with your
mother, not with Nusrat, not even really with Arjun. I hate you
for that.*

*Today I went for a recruitment session with Goldman Sachs and
saw an Indian guy. He was short, balding, dressed in really tight pants
and had a little teapot of a belly from which a black hair curled out
between the buttons of his shirt. But he was also the only guy who
was funny. He took off his tie halfway through the presentation and
tied it around his waist like a cummerbund. He spoke well. His air
of irony about working for Goldman Sachs went down very well
with a crowd of liberal arts students because all of us felt slightly
ashamed for being there.*

*It was your brother. Sammy Ghosh. Will you be offended if I say
that I detested him on sight? Anyway, what does it matter. It's not
like you're ever going to write back. I don't even know if you get the
letters. Maybe your parents hide them from you. Your family may be
a lot more cogent than mine but at least I make my own decisions.
I've been making my own decisions for some time now, Tania.*

*Anyway, the Goldman Sachs recruitment session was the most
waited-for session in the recruitment calendar. Everyone wants to*

*apply to Goldman Sachs, everyone wants to work there. I don't care particularly if it's Goldman Sachs or JP Morgan or Bear Stearns or Lehman Brothers. I just want to be rich. A marble bathroom that's only mine.*

*And don't you dare judge me, Tania Ghosh. I work three jobs to pay for things and I'm tired of it. I'm tired of being a dishwasher in the dining hall, the only one who is not part of a high school rehabilitation program. I'm tired of professors looking through me when I serve them canapes. I'm tired of dropping package slips in mail boxes for J Crew Sweaters that cost 98 dollars. It would take me 17 hours of stuffing mail to make enough money for that sweater. I want to be the girl who buys a sweater for 98 dollars and then rejects it because it's the wrong colour. I want to order steak. I want to buy a dress that's not on sale.*

*I'm not going to be my mother. She also worked three jobs to put herself through college and where did it get her?*

*I know Amrita thinks I am selling out although she's too kind to say it. I am selling out. She had introduced me to an old student of hers who now does human rights law in the Bronx. He shares a chilly apartment with three roommates and wears double sweaters at night because heat is expensive. His law school debt is being paid off slowly by the government because she doesn't make enough money to pay it off himself.*

*I know the type. I know the life. Living in the far reaches of cities where everyone looks resigned and the shops have bars on the windows. Or in the middle of nowhere where the only Pakistani food is at a parrot green four-table restaurant called Taj Mahal with Christmas lights illuminating a doped out Rastafarian asking you if you want salad with your meal.*

*I'm not going to be like that. I want to be one of the people who signs a cheque for ten thousand dollars as a security deposit on an apartment that looks out on Central Park. I want to buy a three dollar cup of coffee every day and take a taxi home whenever I want.*

*I want to buy organic juice in glass bottles. My mother will come live with me. We will find a new psychiatrist, buy the best drugs. She will take art classes at NYU. We will go for long walks on the promenade and complain about the heat.*

*Anyway, I wanted to tell you that I went up to Sammy to speak with him and he knew immediately who I was. Which is flattering really. He looked at me and turned away. In front of everyone. My friend asked me why he cut me like that and I told her that he was anti-Pakistani.*

*I'm going to apply to Goldman Sachs and I'm going to get in. And then I'm going to work real hard and I'm going to be real smart and one day I'm going to be the boss of your fat, oily brother.*

*Wait and see, Tania, wait and see.*

*Love,*
*Tanya*

~

August 11, 1992
Bombay

Dear Tanya,

So just FYI you aren't the only one whose country has weird shit going on. All everyone talks about anymore is the BJP. It's damn boring. Yesterday Nusrat told me that an Urdu-medium school near her house was attacked because it had a Pakistan flag. And I was like why do they have a Pakistan flag and she got super mad and said that every green flag is not a Pakistan flag. Like I care.

She doesn't talk about anything else and doesn't want to hear anything about Arjun or school or anything. All she can think about are these stupid political people and their pointless issues. It's damn annoying.

You know what's weird? Nobody phoned me yesterday and no one has phoned me so far today also. Usually I get like six to eight calls a day.

And at school today, Ritu was absent and no one else sat next to me. I mean the last time Ritu was absent there was a fight about who would sit next to me. But today, no one even looked at me when the bell rang. Do you think they didn't notice?

And at lunch, I sat in our usual spot, but no one came and sat with me except Neenee. She was damn happy to have me all to herself. But where was everyone?

Okay I better go, my mom just came home. Just see. It's 10 o'clock at night. Who comes home at this hour? It's not decent. I'd be so pissed if I was my dad. But all he does is make her tea with fresh ginger.

I mean seriously Dad. You never get what you want by being a pushover.

Ciao,
T

~

*August 23, 1992*
*Karachi*

Dear Tania,

Sometimes I wonder if it's possible if your letters are for real. You're blind when it comes to your mother.

Two boys in my class are leaving at the end of the week because of kidnapping threats. That's just in my class. I don't even know how many are leaving from the other classes. There are many. Father Thomas' office is continually full of parents, fathers sweating through designer shirts, mothers fat, perfumed and crying.

The two boys in my class are Humayun and Mohammed T. Humayun has been in my class since nursery school. He's not very clever but he's very, very sweet. I don't know Mohammed T very well but apparently his family is "involved" with MQM. He's flying out immediately. He doesn't even have a school to go to in America. He's going to go stay with his aunt and uncle in New Jersey and apply from there. I wonder how this will affect his college applications.

I did something bad today. I destroyed Navi's squash racket. He left it on the stairs again and I picked it up, took it to my room and cut the strings. I've told him many times not to leave his racket on the stairs. My mother doesn't really look where she's going. I don't want to imagine what would happen if she tripped on it and fell. She has no meat left on her body.

When Navi saw the cut strings of the racket, he grabbed my shoulders and shook me so hard I bit into my tongue. I have welts on my arms. I love looking at them in the mirror. Dark blushes slowly turning purple.

But I hadn't known that Navi has a club championship coming up. If only I had money, I would buy him a new racket. I'll ask Ali to look in their sports room. Can you believe they have a whole room filled with sports equipment? There's a brand new scuba diving outfit in there. Every time I go in there I wrap the arms of the suit around my head and smell the rubber. It always smells new and promising.

I fought with Ali today. He won't work on his college applications, he won't take the kidnapping threats seriously, he barely takes me seriously. He and Chhoti Bibi have taken to playing cards together although they use beans instead of money because Chhoti Bibi says gambling is un-Islamic. Today neither of them even looked up when I came into the room. I asked Chhoti Bibi to make me tea and she looked up and said, 'Now?'

Can you imagine?

I said, 'Yes, now.'

She got up and left in a huff. Then Ali said to me in a grieved tone that I was not being cool.

Not being cool, I snapped at him. What's not cool is for my boyfriend to come to my house and hang out with my servant.

He just got up and left. He didn't take his stuff and didn't even wear his shoes. He just left. Who leaves without shoes?

I felt bad immediately. As soon as I had said that to him I felt bad. And I felt bad for making Chhoti Bibi go and make me tea.

But I wanted tea. Should I not ask for tea because she's busy? Bibi should have said something to her. Should I say something to Bibi?

Now Chhoti Bibi is not talking to me. She came with the tea, saw that Ali had gone and stormed out. With my tea.

I feel like I'm losing her. She isn't studying at all. Whatever little attention I had before is gone and that I can lay at Ali's door. He laughs at me when I try to get her to study. Why are you forcing her to study, Tanya? I want to play cards with her.

And she sits there grinning like a Cheshire cat.

Ali doesn't understand. He could go his whole life without lifting a finger and it wouldn't matter, he would still have his big houses and servants and tickets to London on demand.

It's not like that for Chhoti Bibi. I'm trying to give her a life and she doesn't even understand it. Her world right now has only one door and she has already stepped through it. But what if there is another door? What if she does really well in the exam and gets into college?

You and I are both living with the choices our mothers made. You don't have to worry about which college you go to, you ask for a phone in your room and you have it, your brother goes to Princeton, paying full tuition and flies home twice a year. I have nightmares of not getting financial aid and I've said no to two birthday parties because I didn't want to ask for money to buy presents.

Ali can't sway me but he sways Chhoti Bibi. She is dazzled by his attention, the way he has of interacting with every single person as if there are no strings, no tags. She looks different with him than she does with me. As if she is a friend.

He has left behind his college applications. Deadlines are coming up and he hasn't even started his essays. His mind is not wired differently, it's not wired at all.

Love,
Tanya

~

*September 1, 1992*
*Bombay*

Dear Tanya,

Did you know my mother used to smoke? And play tennis? There's a picture of her and your mother in bikinis. They're at a pool and it's sunny in the picture and they're laughing at something we can't see.

Some of the stuff in your letters I don't get at all. It's like a movie. And then there's other stuff that's like from my life. I broke something once.

It was a prize my brother had won in an inter-school debate competition and I just hated it so much. It was an ugly blue plate and it said his name on it in big letters, even bigger than the name of our school. Anyway, it wasn't even a first prize, it was a third prize. One night, when my mom was yelling at me because I got a C in Geography, I picked it up and threw it against the wall.

Man she was mad! She just kept yelling and yelling. That's the worst when she does that. The WORST. Her face gets red and her voice is louder than everything else. The plate was sitting there smirking at me. It was almost like self-defence. I picked it up and smashed it.

It felt awesome and I don't regret it one bit. I wish I still had the plate so I could smash it again and again and again. But man my mom lost it that night. A piece of glass from the plate nicked her face and there was like a small drop of blood. She just lost it. She started hitting me like a crazy person. And shit, my mom knows how to hit. My dad had to drag her off me and almost like carry her into their bedroom.

So I get why you cut the strings on your brother's racket. I totally get it.

Anyway so today my mom hit me again. I mean I knew it was coming because I was going to tell her that I refused to write the applications to go to college in America. So I knew she was going to hit me. I was like prepared for it.

And the weird thing is that I am just so damn tired of being sad about Arjun that I was almost looking forward to it. Like if I could stop thinking about Arjun for even a minute, it would be a good thing. He keeps going away and away and away and there's nothing I can do and I've tried like everything. He just keeps leaving.

So yeah I was kind of like looking forward to the fight. I even wanted her to hit me so I'd feel something else.

And it started just like I had imagined it. I went into her study and she was sitting at her desk, frowning at the computer. I told her I wanted to talk to her. She didn't even turn around. I told her I wasn't going to do the college applications because

I didn't want to go to college in America. Then she turned around. She took off her glasses and rubbed her eyes and said in this slow, clear voice as if I am a five-year-old child and that of course I am.

No I'm not, I said. I won't do the applications. You can't make me.

Then she began to yell. Still just sitting in her chair and yelling at me. How I'm stupid and ungrateful and don't know what's good for me. How I waste my time on sports and friends and Arjun and how she's worked so hard for me her whole life and this is how I repay her.

And I was like mom you don't work hard for me you work hard for yourself. You love your job!

And that made her even madder and she started on the Sammy train. Sammy did this and Sammy did that and why can't you be like him and why can't you work hard like him and why can't you why can't you.

I said Sammy is a selfish, boring prick and I don't want to be like him.

I think it was the word prick.

She came at me suddenly and gave me one across my head. Really hard. I fell.

And then suddenly there was a godawful noise which only I recognised as Nusrat screaming as we heard her flying across the house.

Man, that girl can run. She threw herself on top of me.

She covered my face with her hands and her body was on top of mine so that my mother couldn't hit me anymore.

My mom stopped. She just stopped. She stopped shouting and she stopped hitting me. I think she was embarrassed because of Nusrat. She just glared at both of us and then went away. I heard her bedroom door slam and then the shower come on full force. That's what my mom does when she's really mad. She cleans herself.

The funny thing is that Nusrat and I didn't get up. We just lay there on the floor. She was soft and warm on top of me. It felt really nice. It felt like peaceful. I get why little kids just lie down on the floor when they're mad. The floor doesn't say anything. It's just there.

I don't know how it happened but somehow Nusrat's arm was around me and mine was around hers. I could feel her breast under my head and it felt nice. So soft. She was stroking my hair and making weird little noises softly. We lay like that until it got dark and she had to go home.

My mom never came out of her room.

I want my mom to love me like Nusrat loves me. I don't want to have to be Sammy. I don't remember the last time my mom gave me a hug. When I was little she used to hug me all the time. She used to bathe me in her bathroom and I remember feeling so excited to be near her but also terrified of the shampoo going into my eyes. She would hold me between her knees so I couldn't move and there was the cold water of the bath and the hot water of my tears and my mom's hands big and strong on me. I used to feel like I had become part of my mom and even with the shampoo in my eyes I loved it.

How come Nusrat loves me and my mother doesn't love me? My mother doesn't even know all the bad stuff about me. She doesn't know half the shit I've let Arjun do to me. Nusrat knows everything and yet she loves me a lot. I think she loves me even more than her mother and even more than her father.

My mom hasn't spoken to me in six days. She doesn't even look at me. So it didn't really help to feel sad about something else. It's like double sadness.

I'm so tired. I'm so tired of being sad. I wish I could stop feeling. I wish I could just lie on the floor and become like the floor. Cool, silent. Impossible to hurt and impossible to be hurt by.

Love,
Tania

PS—Nusrat's hands are really soft. But her arms are very strong. Isn't that amazing?

## 10

*May 15, 1996*
*New York, NY*

*Dear Tania,*

   *It's spring! It's spring, it's spring! I cannot begin to tell you what it means to live here in New York and have it become spring. Interminable, hateful winter with its snowdrifts and insidious wind chills that creep around like snipers, taking aim and destroying what little warmth you've accumulated through the day.*

   *Even my mother loves spring. The times she has been happy, really quite happy, have all happened in spring. Once it was when she was with Richard, a man she dated for a few months. But the other two times it was nothing specific at all, she was just happy. It was just spring*

   *It has taken me twenty years to ask my mother how she met my father. I had gone to Boston for my twentieth birthday and she had taken me out for breakfast to her favourite diner. She was laughing over the seeds of the honeydew melon that had dripped by mistake into her coffee. I snapped a picture of her on my camera.*

   *Her smile wobbled when I asked her and she looked out of the window at the newly budding trees until I thought she wasn't going to say anything. Then she said that they had been the best years of her life. When she had met my father and they had fallen in love and got married. Had Navi and me.*

*It's an ordinary story. They met at a friend's party. My father was the awkward, brilliant scientist about to graduate and go to medical college. My mother was the elegant, quiet summa cum laude, Phi Beta Kappa, head of her class, on a full scholarship, first generation college-goer. Both of them only children of quiet, unambitious people who didn't quite know how to respond to their children's singular love and determination to be together.*

*My mother's parents hadn't wanted her to move to Pakistan of course. She had only been thirty-three years old. Thirty-three with a Pakistani husband and six-year-old twins moving to a new world. I wonder if she had thought it was an experiment.*

*I told her I think my father has Asperger's. She looked at me blankly and then laughed. 'Your father is just a selfish man, Tanya.' When I was leaving the next day, she hugged me and said, 'Don't worry, Tanya, there's nothing wrong with your father.'*

*But that's not what I wanted to hear. I wanted a secret that would make it all make sense. I wanted there to be a reason. Some brain asymmetry. The tiniest droplet of neurotransmitter going the wrong way, a childhood accident that damaged something deep inside the cranium where no one can see. Something outside of his control.*

*My therapist says I need to love myself before I can let anyone love me. But that's not strictly true, is it? From your first letter, I wanted you to love me.*

*If I could go back, I would undo everything. And I would start by asking you straight out, no doubts, no hesitations, just a straight question—Tania, do you love me?*

*Tania, did you love me?*

*Love,*
*Tanya*

*September 11, 1992*
*Karachi*

Dear Tania,

It finally happened last night.

It's seven in the morning and I'm waiting for Salman Bhai to come drive Navi and me to school. The sun has come up and is shining through the gulmohur tree outside my window, throwing dancing shadows on my bed. The gardener is watering the plants and downstairs I can hear a low buzz from the kitchen where Bibi is telling Chhoti Bibi what to cook for lunch. There's a mad bird in the trees calling out its avian magnum opus as if it must, as if it has to, as if it will die if it doesn't. I can see the maid in the house next door, down on her haunches, wiping the floor with a wet cloth. Wet swathes of red floor form concentric circles around her feet. Any minute now Salim Bhai will be here, walking up the slope to our house with a faded backpack that used to be ours, with its tiny Mickey Mouse sticker in the corner that he has not seen or has decided to keep.

I don't want to go to school today.

You know what I'm going to tell you. You must know. I've known it was going to happen to us from the minute I found out about Musti's brother. And now Musti is going to a boarding school in England with hot water only on weekends and poor, darling, stupid Musti, a fish out of water, a Karachi boy out of Pakistan.

For us it came in the middle of the night which is different from the times it came for Musti (in the morning), for Azim (in the evening) and the boy who was killed (noon). Why was he killed? I must look into it. Put together a file to present to my disbelieving father.

But why did they come to us in the middle of the night? I've been thinking about that. Does that mean they are scared to show us who they are? Does that mean that they are people we know?

A stentorian banging on the door at 3:30 in the morning. I leaped out of dreams and bed, knowing.

I tried my mother's door on my way down but it was locked. For once, I didn't want to open it.

My father came down the stairs at the same time I did, tying around himself a very old robe I remember from America. A memory of throwing up on it once when I had been sick. Do you think it still smells? I remember my mother telling me once that child vomit is the worst smell in the world. Isn't it funny that throughout the whole thing, I never stood close enough to my father to smell his dressing gown?

Chhoti Bibi and Bibi in the living room, holding hands. Bibi looking scared and for the first time, old. Hair almost all white now and very little of it left. Wrinkles I had never seen before lit by the blazing of all the lights downstairs. Our living room never this bright and suddenly quite shabby. Walls with damp patches, a hole in the wall above the sideboard where once there had been a beautiful tricone lantern twisted together with bronze grape leaves. Chhoti Bibi composed, clear-eyed. Standing back from opening the door only because Bibi was holding both her hands.

And through it all, a wild, desperate smashing of a fist on the front door. Beneath it, between the hard thuds, the sound of someone weeping.

My father opened the door and our nightwatchman fell in, stumbling into my father's arms. The entire front of his uniform was bloody. I heard an intake of breath behind me. Navi stood on the landing of the stairs, wearing only his underwear, his body alight in goosebumps, his arms hugging himself so hard that his fingers may have clasped behind his back.

I still don't know what he's thinking. Even now. What do you think he's thinking, Tania? What is my twin brother thinking?

It took ages to calm the watchman. I saw a side of my father I hadn't seen before. He led him to a chair and made him sit down, pushing him down physically when the watchman wanted to stay in my father's arms. He pulled up a stool and began to clean what I saw were cuts on his face. Under the lights, we saw that his uniform was soaked in blood and incongruously, there were feathers all over it.

The whole time the watchman cried and blubbered, nose running, eyes running, unchecked. He curled up like a child, shrinking from my father's touch, his hands covering his face as if he was being beaten.

They came in the dark and broke the lights outside the watchman's hut. They threw in a half-killed hen that flailed around the windowless shed, pecking at the watchman, I don't know why because no one, not even a hen could have been scared of this man.

Why did the hen do that? Did it think it was the watchman who had injured it? Maybe it was just looking for companionship before death. I've been thinking about this. What do you think, Tania?

Then the men came back (he couldn't tell us how many) and cut off the hen's neck. They gave the watchman a piece of paper wrapped around a stone with string.

The watchman took out the stone. It looked so ordinary, Tania. Cheap school notebook paper lined with double green lines, splotches of blood and brown string.

My father knocked the stone out of the watchman's hand and made Chhoti Bibi go and get surgical gloves from the table. He put them on carefully, calmly, all of it so calm as if this happens every day.

It was just a single sheet of paper. It had my brother's weekly schedule on it, by the hour, by the day. The mornings he leaves early for squash, the days he goes to the club for cheese pakodas and hard-boiled eggs after school and tennis. The days he is in school until late at night, playing football and then going to the houses of friends whose addresses are also written out neatly with phone numbers.

That's it. Nothing else.

Tell me Tania, was the hen scared?

My father picked up the phone.

'Papa, we can't go to the police.'

He looked at me with a frown on his face. As if he couldn't remember exactly where I came from. I felt an inclination to introduce myself. Hello, I am Tanya, your daughter. Please don't call the police because they will kill your son, my brother.

'Of course we have to go to the police.'

'You can't go to the police!' With a loud smash, Chhoti Bibi put down the tray of teacups she was carrying and grabbed my father's arm. I think he was stunned into silence.

'You can't go to the police,' she said again, shaking his arm for emphasis. 'They killed that other boy who went to that other school.'

'Not because they called the police!' said Navi looking up from his silent, intense contemplation of the watchman who had, as if in a cartoon, fallen asleep and was snoring lightly. 'Because his dad wasn't giving money to the party.'

Chhoti Bibi looked distraught. She has an inexplicable but terrifying fear of the police that I've never fully understood. She stood there with braids erupting from all over her head, each tied neatly in her trademark fluorescent pink ribbon, her chest heaving, looking from my father to my brother as they spoke in English, trying desperately to understand. In that moment I loved Chhoti Bibi so much it physically hurt. Who was this many-winged girl who had come into my family and decided to love us?

But now, in the light of day, I'm not so sure it's love. She went to sleep afterwards. Listen to her now, singing tunelessly along with her beloved radio. If that's love, it has a very short memory.

My father and Navi were discussing the logistics of how the threat could have been dropped off. None of the other threats had been dropped off in this way, in the middle of the night, with a dead hen. Some had been posted, some had come with a street boy, paid to walk up and ring the doorbell or hand it over to the watchman like a hand-delivered wedding invitation. Others received phone calls. Why hadn't we received a phone call, my father asked Navi?

'Our phone has been disconnected for two weeks now,' I said.

My father looked at me. Again that faintly puzzled expression.

'We haven't paid the bill. I asked you for the money and you said you'd take care of it.'

A look of annoyance flitted on my father's face, making him look for a brief moment, like Navi when, as children, I would find him in a game of hide-n-seek.

'Ours is different because we are different and you know why.'

My father and Navi both looked like I had scalded them.

'I said we are never going to talk about that.' My father's voice was low and angry.

'We've received a kidnapping threat. I'm talking about it.'

I don't know the full details but many years ago, we had received another threat. It said something bad about my father marrying a kafir, a non-believer and how he would be punished for it. The funny thing is my father is not a believer himself, not in the Muslim way of things. He is Parsi. But whoever sent the note didn't know that. The police had told my parents that we would have to be extra vigilant, especially during bad times.

'It's not a kidnapping threat,' said Navi. 'It just has my schedule on it.'

'Don't be stupid!' My father and I said together.

There was the sound of a door closing upstairs. My mother had come out of her room and stood holding the railing of the stairs, looking impossibly frail. I wanted to go to her and shepherd her back to her room but I felt so tired. I couldn't get up from the step where I was sitting. I couldn't stop what was going to happen. I couldn't save her or him.

I admit now that I didn't even want to try.

'What has happened?' said my mother, coming down the stairs slowly, holding the railing with both her hands. I saw the silhouette of her legs as she stepped past me. Long, thin and white, they trembled.

She looked from my father to Navi and asked again, 'What has happened?'

My father hid his hand with the note behind his back. Why did he do that? Did he have some idea of saving her from it?

'What is that?'

No one answered her.

She found her way to a sofa, holding on to things. I felt as if I had left my body and was circling above. Her impossible thinness, the teeter of her legs, the way her hands looked like claws as they gripped the edges of things. My father standing hunched by the window, his eyes trapped and angry. Navi, sullen and unsure. Neither of them seeing how frail she had become. Both of them obstinately stuck in their own worlds, obstinately blind.

My mother tried to get up again to take the piece of paper from my father. I couldn't stand it anymore, I took it from my father and shoved it into her hands.

She looked at it, her thin eyebrows merging, her forehead stapling, her mouth slowly opening and forming an O. Her hands started to tremble. Then they started to shake. Then the paper fell out of her hands and we could see her eyes, filling with tears, her hands shaking so hard, she put them under her thighs where they made them hop softly.

'What is this?'

'It's nothing, Lisa.'

'It's not nothing!' Again I didn't speak alone, this time the words came out of Navi and me, in the same time, each word and space at the same time.

'It will blow over,' said my father. 'It's a prank. We'll call the police and they will find the jokers.'

I was willing Navi to look at me but he was sitting on the floor, his head between his hands.

'Jamshed.' My mother said finally. My father's name sounded rusty in her mouth. 'Jamshed, we have to go.'

'Go to the police?' He looked at her hopefully as if he was working a tricky fuse and any moment the lights would come on.

'No Jamshed. Go home.'

If I had to find a single moment when my family stopped being a family, it would be that moment. Although if you asked me when that moment started, I wouldn't be able to tell you. Had it started when they met? When they moved to Pakistan? When he started the hospital? When she started getting sad? When they stopped paying attention to us?

Why did they stop paying attention to us?

One day I will ask my mother what my father was like when she met him. Had he been charming? Had he been attentive? Had he been interested?

From then on, the conversational was eerily close to my fantasies of moving back to America.

My father said: leave Pakistan, how foolish, how unheard of, how can anyone ever leave pristine Pakistan especially with his hospital now in it?

My mother said: stay in Pakistan with this threat on the life of their son, how could he suggest that, did it not matter, did nothing matter other than his bloody hospital that she hated with a passion and hoped would burn down?

My father said: she didn't support him, had never supported him, had never wanted to move here, had never fully moved here, if only she would make an effort things would be better.

My mother said: He didn't love anyone, had never loved anyone, not even Navi and she had always thought that at least he had loved Navi. (She didn't look at me when she said that. Neither did my father. I felt Navi's gaze on me but I couldn't look up. I felt ashamed.)

My father said: The hospital was almost done, things would get better, this was just an idle threat, she didn't understand, she wasn't from here.

My mother stopped speaking. She sat there looking at nothing, holding Navi's hand in hers.

In my fantasies when I had imagined moving back to America, my mother never cried. In my fantasies, my mother just won. In my fantasies, my father softened and put his arm around us and said, okay my darlings, if the whole family wants to move back to America then we will move back to America. Sometimes in my fantasies, we went out for pizza and ice cream to celebrate. Sometimes in my fantasies, my parents kissed and held hands. Once, during a particularly lurid My Little Pony phase, we all flew back to America on lavender horses with luggage tied to their hair.

But never in my fantasies did my mother say, 'It's America or divorce.' Never in my fantasies did my father grow cold like stone and say, 'As you wish, Lisa. Who the hell am I to stop you.' Never in my fantasies was there a blood-dotted piece of paper on the table with every detail of my brother's life plotted out like a spider web.

Never in my fantasies did my mother, father and brother not even see me leave the room.

Everything is quiet again. My mother is back in her room, having done her damage, like a small, deadly lizard I once saw in a National Geographic video. My father is at the hospital.

Did I ever tell you we live in a beautiful house? It has pillars all along the front with a red verandah that runs all the way around the house. There's a large garden in front and an even larger garden at the back. We have lovely gardens.

In the mornings before school, I almost love this house. The quiet, the early sunlight, the sound of the birds, the mist from the gardener's hosepipe, the slap of wet cloth on the car as Salman Bhai cleans it for the day.

I don't know what's going to happen to us, Tania. Please don't stop writing to me. I don't know what's going to happen to me.

Love,
Tanya

~

*September 21, 1992*
*Bombay*

My life is over Tanya. My life is completely over. I mean I get that big shit is going on in your life but my life is over.

He told everyone. He told everyone at school. Everyone knows. That's why no one is talking to me. And I know him, I know him so well, I know he made it sound bad, I know he made it sound cheap. I bet you anything he told the guys I swallowed. I bet you he told them he fucked me from behind.

He took that night away from me.

I am beyond emotion. Neenee told me. Today at lunch when I asked her to sit with me she said she couldn't and I laughed at her and she told me. There was pity in her eyes. Pity in Neenee's eyes. For me. I hate her. I hate him. I hate everyone. I can't breathe.

Someone wrote slut in the back of my Hindi notebook today. It was really tiny and in capitals. In P.E. when I did a triple somersault, someone whispered, 'You can see her cunt.'

Arjun wasn't in school. I went to his house after school but no one opened the door. I heard giggling inside. Him and his chutiya building friends.

I can't believe it. I can't believe it. Twelve years of hard work gone in a flash. I OWNED this school. Now I'm nothing. I'm worse than nothing. I'm a slut. I'm the girl who had sex with a guy who is not even her boyfriend.

I can't think. I can't feel. I am going to buy a ticket and come to Karachi. I can't stay here. I will die if I stay here.

Send me your address. I'm coming.

Tania

# 11

*Dear Tania,*

*You had once told me that if something can happen to anyone in the world it can happen to you. The nightmares are back.*

*Last night I dreamt of Nusrat. In my dream she was in New York with me. We were walking down Broadway in the early 1900s after the university blocks end and before the posh blocks begin. I told her to hold my hand because it's not a safe part of the city. But she kept running away. She kept running into dreary buildings with steel jaildoor entrances and I kept saying, that's a homeless shelter Nusrat, that's a homeless shelter, come out of there.*

*But I couldn't find her. There was a snowstorm. I couldn't see her anymore. I shouted for her and shouted for her. There was a man leering at the entrance of one of the shelters. I knew that Nusrat was in there and that I had to go in and get her but the man was frightening and the building was frightening. And the snow kept falling, really fast, really silent until my feet were buried and then my legs and I was drowning and choking in the snow when I woke up.*

Thankfully it is no longer winter and I no longer have to clutch at the heater to get warm. In fact, I opened the window and jumped out and sat outside in the grass for a little while, looking up at the stars. I like to imagine that those same stars look down on you.

I got the job at Goldman. It's a pretty big deal Tania, only four people got offers from my year and the other three are white frat boys whose fathers work on Wall Street. I'm going to hear a lot of talk about tokenism on the one hand and rich international students stealing away opportunities from minority American students on the other. Let them think I'm rich. I like it.

You know what I'm going to do with my signing bonus? I'm going to buy first class tickets for my mother and me to go to India. We will go to Delhi and see the Red Fort and Humayun's tomb and Jaipur and Agra and the Taj Mahal. My mother wants to do an Ayurveda stay in Kerala. I want to go to Goa.

Your mother is coming to meet my mother. I might go to the Andaman Islands when she comes. It is always uncomfortable when she calls to speak to my mother and I pick up the phone. She starts to ask me about classes, about Columbia, about my job search and she abruptly stops. I wait for her to finish her question, finish her sentence and then I realize she isn't going to.

Just so you know, I have never asked her any questions. And she hasn't told me anything. But she has been a really good friend to my mother. I often wonder what it is that my mother gives her. Maybe it's just nice to have someone who allows you to take care of her. Your mother, unexpectedly, has a lot of tenderness. My mother is unresisting of your mother's tenderness.

Do you have someone like my mother in your life? Who do you give yourself to? Your bony wit and sudden squalls. Your unexpected wells of empathy. It could have been me. It should have been me.

*Do you know how hard it is to be the person responsible for the life you're living? Every day I wake up and regret that one day, that one evening when everything had gone wrong and I didn't stop myself from writing that one letter, from taking it out to the post office and watching the impassive woman behind the counter stamp the envelope and drop it in a large metal bin?*

*I want to make something of my life, Tania. I'm not yet a whole person but I'm trying to be. That must mean something.*

*Then why do I feel like none of it will matter until I have your blessing? Is it because I know I will never have it?*

*Love,*
*Tanya*

~

*October 2, 1992*
*Bombay*

Dear Tanya,

If something can happen to someone in this world, it can totally happen to you. That's what I've learnt over the last few days in school. If someone had told me that I would one day be treated like this at school I would have laughed in their face.

But it has totally come true. I am the opposite of popular, I am the most despised person in the class. Well, to be honest not the whole class. Ever since this happened and people stopped sitting with me and stopped letting me sit in the best seats at the back, I've realised that there are other people in my school, even in my class. I just never noticed them before.

I don't regret that night one bit. No matter how he acts now I know what he was like with me. I know that he crawled into my arms and cried like a baby (I mean literally like a baby because he was like all squashed into my boobs, it was a little weird) and no matter what he says now, I know he loved me that night. And I loved him. I'm not ashamed.

But my life is shit. It's a slow meanness. No one says anything mean directly to my face. Actually no one says anything to me at all. I wasn't picked to play basketball in P.E. class and I am the basketball captain. Stupid girls, girls like Parul and Mona who have never had any lift, who never even *tried* to call me on the phone, are the worst. I can almost see them drooling in triumph. I guess small people like it when big people fall. But it's not clever. If they were really clever, they would be my friends now. Because when a girl has been the most popular girl in school for twelve years she'll be back.

Because obviously I'm going to be back. This is temporary. This will blow over. I'll do something really cool. The Gymnastics championships are next week so that'll be good because I look really hot in a leotard. Boys are too dumb to play politics for too long. And soon the girls will be bored with it. Life is more exciting with me in than out of it.

But from now on I'll be a cool girl who did 'bad stuff' even if people forget the details of what the bad stuff was. Everywhere I go, there'll be an invisible reputation attached and sometimes it will enter rooms and meet people before I will. It's funny. Arjun has made me a girl version of him.

But I'm not going to talk about him. I am never going to talk to him or talk about him again. He is dead. So don't bring him up in your letter, don't ask about him, nothing.

What's going on in your house? How is your mother doing? What have they decided about Navi?

Listen, if you like need money you can borrow from me. I mean of course. I get quite a bit of pocket money. And I have an insane number of CDs and I like don't listen to most of them anymore. You can get good money for them at this shop I know.

I have no idea how to send it to you or whatever but you're the clever one, you'll figure it out. But just saying. We don't have to tell anyone.

Love,
Tania

~

*October 12, 1992*
*Karachi*

Dear Tania,

I don't want your money. If you offer again I will stop writing to you.

I'm sorry Arjun did that to you. I'm not surprised but I'm sorry.

Chhoti Bibi gave the exam. I went with her. She came out before the time was up for every exam. She said cheerfully that she answered only four of the questions in Math. She's convinced me she did fantastically in Urdu and says she's pretty sure she has passed in all the other subjects. I asked her if she felt good about having done it and she turned to me in the car and said, Baji, do *you* feel good?

What a ridiculous question.

And then, believe it or not, she promptly forgot all about it. I have no idea what she's done with the books, they've disappeared from my room and she hasn't once asked when the results will be out. (They will be out in a month.) She positively glows when she joins Bibi in front of the living room TV in the evening to watch soap operas. Clearly she misses studying very much.

My mother is in a strange state of opposites. One day she is resolute and flies around the house taking down pictures and giving instructions and calling movers and the next day she sinks into silence and can't get out of bed. I never know which day it's going to be when I wake up. I'm so glad it's Eid holidays because I can be at home.

No, my parents haven't talked.

Navi has been sent off to stay with my Dadi in Murree. Until…until they figure out what to do? I don't know. I miss Navi. I didn't think it was possible but I do. Even when he wasn't in the house, he was someone else living here other than my father and mother. Now there's just the three of us. It highlights my mother's bouts of frenetic activity and it amplifies my father's continued silence.

I'm pretty deep into my applications. I've sent off Harvard and Stanford. I'm working on the others. I don't suppose I should ask you how yours are going. You're making a big mistake, Tania. This is not just about the next four years, you know, it's the rest of your life. Besides, with everything going on, don't you dream of escaping?

Love,
Tania

~

*October 20, 1992*
*Bombay*

Dear Tanya,

Don't you get it? For me escaping will be to not go to college in America!

I'm getting scared man. Things are still bad at school. It's been two weeks now. I thought they'd get bored. But they're just getting meaner. I wasn't invited to Soumya's birthday party or

Shaival's weekend thing at Marvae. But the meanest thing was I had gone to Cellars with my cousin from Delhi and when we got there everyone from school was there. And they just ignored me. Looked right through me as if I didn't exist. I wanted to cry so badly but I wasn't going to give them the satisfaction. Besides once you show weakness it's over. Permanently. So I just grabbed my cousin's hand and we danced and danced and danced and danced. But every song, every move, I was watching them. I was waiting for them to come to me. But although they looked at me many many times and I know they were wondering who my cousin was, not a single one of them did.

I've grown up with these people. I'm in every picture of every birthday party Soumya has had since she was born. Until the day of her party, I thought she was going to call me. I had imagined how it would be, she would call me in whispers and say I can't talk but obvers you must come ya. And I'd laugh to show no hard feelings and say that I had another party to go to but happy birthday and I'd stop by for some cake.

I got into a fight with Nusrat today because she got all preachy and was like oh these are not real friends. When I told her she didn't understand, she got super huffy and wrote in her notebook that she understands a lot more because she can't speak because all she can do is listen. She's so sensitive man.

Anyway, I had meant to call you but it got super late and I'm damn scared your dad will pick up the phone. He sounds British man. I'll call you tomorrow. Maybe I'll have better news on how things are at school tomorrow.

Love,
T

~

*October 31, 1992*
*Karachi*

Dear Tania,

A boy was killed. Can you believe it? A boy was kidnapped and then killed. The family was putting together the ransom but time had run out and the boy was killed.

He was seventeen years old. His name was Shahid. He had a stammer and he played inter-school squash. He went to St. Mary's School for Boys. He played against Navi last year.

My mother tore the article out in the newspaper and went and banged loudly on my father's door. She stood there in a crumpled nightie with egg stains on the front, greasy hair, trembling lip, eyes red from crying, banging on her husband's door to be heard.

My father wasn't home.

The funeral is tomorrow. The flag flew at half mast in our school today and when I looked around at the different classes all lined up, they seem to have shrunk. Far fewer boys than there used to be. Quite a few of the students were crying. Some of the teachers were crying too. Even the men.

He was seventeen years old. Apparently he was quite the bad boy. Used to do a lot of drugs. He was also applying to go to college in America. Did decently in the SATs—1320. That's 100 more than what Ali got. But Ali is an artistic genius. He doesn't do well on tests.

Navi called today to ask me to send him his cricket bat and soccer cleats. He has found some kind of sports club there. I thought it would feel really good to hear his voice but when I heard it I only felt vastly irritated. I wanted to tell him that there was an update: that Mom had made up her mind, that Chhoti Bibi had passed her exam, that my father was spending more time at home. But I could tell him nothing except that his old squash rival had been killed.

In Assembly today, someone asked loudly how come they don't kidnap girls. It was a Class 8 boy. No one answered him.

Love,
Tanya

~

*November 7, 1992*
*Bombay*

Dear Tania,

Holy crap man. They killed a kid? I mean I know you weren't making all this up but I never thought it would actually happen. That's insane. Good thing your brother has been sent away. Nusrat looked up Murree in the Atlas. It looks far. Of course you miss him.

Anyway, so I have no happy news to cheer you up. Things are really bad. My mom is worse than mad that I don't want to go to college in America. She's like SAD.

She thinks I don't respect her because I don't want to go to her college and I don't want to follow her path. It's not like that. I can't help that I'm made differently. Sammy wants her path. But you know what I realized? She wants me to want her path.

And that made me think. Did Sammy know that? Is that why he is following her path? And how come I don't want to? And what about my dad? Does it make him feel bad that it's all about my mom? He's never once said anything about wanting us to be accountants.

My family is so weird Tanya. All the talking, all the shouting and yet there's so much stuff that's underneath that is never said. Are we all constantly trying to be something else to please someone? And for what?

I wanted my mother to hug me. I was crying and I wanted her to put her arms around me and say it's okay. But she just stood there, leaning against the window. She asked me to leave. I didn't go. She took the car keys and left the house.

Nusrat came and found me and took me to the servant's room which is a balcony to hang wet clothes. She hugged me, she held me, she kissed me. I stayed there for a long time after she left, wrapped in my mom's gold and yellow sari that I pulled down from the clothesline. I wanted to take that wet sari to bed with me, I wanted to wrap it around myself and sleep in it but I didn't because I knew it would make my mom mad.

Nusrat hasn't come all week. There are like a lot of disruptions going on in the city so I guess that's why. Morchas and naka bandis every day. A morcha is when there are lots of people out on the road looking angry and chanting stuff together. A naka bandi is when they stop all the cars on the road. It makes the traffic like insane. The trains have been running late and the teachers have all be coming late to school and leaving early.

Is this what your life is like? Not having people to talk to in school? Not having anyone call you when you get home? Not having someone to call at eleven o'clock at night and go get ice cream with? I'm sorry man. I didn't know.

I still don't know what's going to happen. Is my mom going to allow me to stay in Bombay? Or is she going to pretend like I never said anything and just make me apply anyway? I can totally see that. I can see her coming into my room (without knocking) with another application to another college she hadn't thought of before. And it will be like I had never said anything.

I miss Nusrat. Maybe she will come tomorrow.

Love,
Tania

~

*November 15, 1992*
*Karachi*

Dear Tania,

CHHOTI BIBI FAILED. By 20 marks. She got 55 in the Social Sciences, 60 in Urdu, 30 in English and 12 in Math. TWELVE. Who gets 12 in Math? Is that even a number that is possible to get in an exam? Out of 100?

And believe it or not, she is furious at me for going and getting the marks. She tried to grab it from me but luckily for her, I was able to prevent it. It's locked in my drawer. What is wrong with her? 12 in Math? 30 in English? My face was burning.

And instead of apologising, instead of feeling bad, she's angry with me? She's asking me how I have the right to pick up her marksheet for her? Who didn't even know that the word marksheet existed until a few months ago? Forget about gratitude, she's mad. She's mad.

I was so upset when I saw it, Tania. I really thought she was going to pass (and that I could put it on my remaining applications. This is the sole reason why I haven't sent out my Harvard application yet.) I was going to go buy samosas and kachoris and jalebis and mithai to celebrate. I was going to take her shopping in a mall. I had asked my mother for money for it. My mother had smiled at me and kissed my head. It was one of her 'I'm leaving and I love it' days.

Anyway, now Chhoti Bibi is acting like I've committed a huge crime. Yes, please forgive me for trying to help you, for trying to give you a better life. It was a terrible, selfish thing to do. I even went to her room to try to talk to her. She was lying on the bed crying. There was nowhere to sit. So I just stood at the door and asked her when she was going to apologise to me. She ignored me. I asked her again, more loudly.

She bounced up on the bed and began to scream in Punjabi and Urdu. I didn't understand all of it but the gist of it was that she had done it all for me and that she had never liked school and she hated studying and she hated exams and I had betrayed her and now she would have to run away and then how would Mohammed go to an English-medium school?

'Why do you have to run away?'

'Because they will now come and catch me.'

'Who?'

She pointed at the window. Outside, the garden was quiet and empty.

The police, she whispered and her face crumpling like a child's, she started crying into her hands.

Something about the way she cried, lustily, with such abandon, reminded me of you, Tania. I thought, when Tania cries, she cries like that. It made me want to comfort Chhoti Bibi.

It took some time to untangle the mess but I finally got to the bottom of her fear of the police. It turns out that the family of her husband-for-a-day had threatened police action when she bit the boy and left him. Chhoti Bibi's family had rubbed this in when she had refused to go back, building up a picture of a police force whose priorities, among dealing with riots and murders and highway robberies is to find Chhoti Bibi and put her in jail.

But why would they want you? I asked her.

She looked through the fingers of her hands in surprise. Why would they not?

She also has a tangled understanding of universities, of the government—of authority, in general, I suppose. It took a lot of patient explanations to convince her that the police is not the paramount authority in the country and that they have nothing to do with universities and schools or anything else really. I'm not sure she fully understood or believes me but at least, by virtue of swearing on the Koran that the police does not know her exam scores, I was able to assure her that the police was not coming to get her because she had failed her exams.

She wiped her eyes and began to make dinner. She got me a stool to sit on while she began to make the dough for rotis.

I don't ever want to live with a man, she said firmly. My father used to beat my mother before he died and then after he died, his brother and his mother beat my mother. My mother was married into this family when she was fourteen years old and has lived with them ever since. She doesn't even know where her own family is anymore.

When I was getting married, my mother went to the mosque and prayed for me to have a husband like her father. My grandfather was a very good man. He never beat my grandmother and he worked very hard and he provided for every single of their nine children. He used to go to the fair every spring and bring back new clothes and toys and fresh, hot jalebis for everyone and he used to love all his children equally, even the girls. He built them a separate toilet with his own hands so they wouldn't have to walk to the fields in winter.

'What if the man you had married was going to be like your grandfather?'

She spat scornfully into the dustbin and pummelled the dough furiously. 'He was the bully of the village,' she said. 'Everyone hated him. We had to go the long way round to get water because he would sit with his idiot friends to say horrible things to us and try to touch us as if we went the short way.'

I pictured him as Hamza, the big bully of my school. I could easily picture Hamza doing all of that.

'Also,' said Chhoti Bibi, 'his family is in a lot of debt. God knows what would have happened if I had stayed with him. They would have definitely taken my jewellery and sold it.'

'Where is your jewellery now?' I asked.

'My mother took it.'

'So you don't have it anyway.'

She looked at me in surprise. 'My mother can have my jewellery.'

Every time I think I understand Chhoti Bibi, she eludes my grasp.

'Baji, do you know how to make rotis?'

I shook my head.

'Then come and learn. You will need to make rotis one day.'

More because I didn't want to go back to my room, more because I liked sitting there with her in the cheerfully lit kitchen with dusk falling outside and a cat meowing somewhere and the blue flame of the stove twinkling, I agreed.

She taught me how to measure the size of the ball and she taught me how to flatten it gently before rolling it flat. She taught me how to dust it lightly, very lightly with flour so that they wouldn't stick. She taught me her secret trick of dipping her little finger in a bowl of oil and rubbing it lightly into the roti before setting it on the tava. She was so happy to teach me, her face glowed with sweat and focus. I realised suddenly that she does have intelligent eyes and somehow in the dimmer light of my room, sitting at my desk while she sat on the floor, dreaming out of the window every time she thought I wasn't looking, I hadn't noticed the quality of her eyes.

She told me that the boy she had been married to had been a real dunce in school. 'Worse than me,' she said, taking a mangled piece of dough from me and rolling it again into a ball. Then she added half proudly, half shyly, 'I was actually not half bad in school.'

'Then why didn't you study here with me?'

'Because I don't want your life!' It came out in a burst with flecks of saliva dotting her mouth. Standing under a fluorescent tube light, she was lit against the darkness of the night sky behind her like a picture of a Hindu goddess I had once seen, glowing in the dark.

She hung her head. 'I want to be Bibi.'

I could only look at her, silent.

She grinned and said, 'Happier. Bibi but happier.'

She made me put my lumpy rotis on the tava. She made me flatten them and smoothen them and flip them over on a low flame.

'Bibi has so much money. She has bought two houses and now, do you know, she makes more in rent from those two houses than she makes here in your house?'

I didn't know.

'Once Bibi retires, I will take over her job. And then I will go get Mohammed from the village. My mother won't mind. She is tired of children.' Chhoti Bibi deftly rescued my slowly burning roti and dropped it on the counter where she had spread a red napkin faded to pink. I remembered that napkin from when I had been in kindergarten. My mother used to wrap it around my tiffin box in which she used to always put grapes, no matter the season. I used to love sitting alone at Break, away from teachers and girls, break open the starched, ironed napkin and expose the luscious green grapes. Grapes were my favourite.

'Besides,' said Chhoti Bibi, 'Mohammed loves me the most in the world. He calls me Chhoti Ammi.'

I burnt my finger on the tava. Chhoti Bibi grabbed it and dunked it roughly into a screw of salt in her hand. I felt the burn numb my finger, the damp warmth of her palm enveloping it.

'I will send Mohammed to an English-medium school,' she said seriously. 'He will have to pass his exams. I will hire tutors.'

Suddenly I felt alone, sitting there on the stool, watching Chhoti Bibi go through the rotis I'd made, discarding, refashioning, selecting, discarding. She turned on the water in the sink and dropped the hot tawa in there, humming tunelessly and frowning as the steam enveloped her. She did not notice when I got up to leave.

I got up and went away to listen at my mother's door as usual. There was an old jazz record she was playing, something she found in one of her manic episodes of 'packing'. She had taken to filling up a glass of whisky with lemon and honey and sipping it through the day.

How stupid I was, Tania. I really thought I was helping Chhoti Bibi. But the whole time she had just been indulging me. She knows exactly what she wants and has always known it, always been confident in it. She was born into a Chhoti Bibi shaped hole in the world and she fills it every day. Do you know what it takes for a seventeen-year-old Pakistani girl to say with such confidence, I don't ever want to marry a man?

How brave she is. How brave Navi is, uprooting his life to go live in my grandmother's house without complaining. All he wants are soccer cleats. How brave is Ali, coming into and out of the everyday world as he pleases, as he wants, never worrying about his future, never worrying about being kidnapped, never worrying about being loved. How brave are you, telling your mother that you don't want to live her dream for you. How brave is Nusrat with her intelligence and self-possession and her burning. How brave are you Tania, to keep going to school in spite of everything. How brave to continue to plot and to plan, resolute in your vision that you will one day regain your throne.

I'm not brave. I'm not brave, Tania. I'm my mother's daughter. We are not brave.

Love,
Tanya

~

*November 22, 1992*
*Bombay*

Dear Tanya,

Dude, you are so intense man. What's with this brave stuff? Is it because I said you weren't brave? I was kidding man. Come on. Snap out of it. And pick up the phone when I call. No one picks up at your house anymore. I swear I was kidding. I mean I know I'm brave but you are too. I mean look at you all ready to leave everything and go off to America. That's brave! I can't do that!

You like won't BELIEVE what happened. Like WON'T BELIEVE it. I can't believe it.

Yesterday, I had called Arjun to my house. I had decided that I needed to do something. I couldn't have him ruining my life like this. It's my life, my city. My school, my people. I've been here forever, I will be here forever. It's like your dad had said right? Sometimes you have to make sacrifices for what you want.

So my plan was to like offer an exchange. I would do stuff for him and then he had to tell everyone that a lot of what was being said was not true. That the stuff he said, the worst of the stuff he said, had all been made up. Which it was. The kind of shit he's said...anyway, no point in going into that now.

He came over thinking I was going to cry. I could see it in the way he walked in. Pretending to be all caring. Oh T, how are you, T baby I miss you...I wanted to puke on him.

I made him come out to the balcony to talk to me because I couldn't stand the thought of him being in my room.

But I was polite. I had to be. I told him my end of the bargain. That he could have six times with me where I would do whatever he wanted if he would tell people that there hadn't been any of the bad stuff. Anything other than what actually happened.

I don't think he had expected me to be so business-like about it. Then he began to negotiate what I would do during the six times. I almost backed out then Tanya, it made me sick to hear him even say those things. Then he said he would think about it. I told him that the offer would expire in a day and if he didn't take it, I would tell everyone he has a tiny penis. 'Don't think,' I told him, 'that I have no power left.'

Then I made him leave because I couldn't stand the smell of his cologne for one more moment. Anyway, then Nusrat and I went to go sit at our spot on the rocks by the sea and I forgot all about it. Well, no, I didn't forget about it but I wasn't thinking about it. Actually I was. I was thinking about the six times and the things I had agreed to. But I was pretending not to.

Today in school, during Econ, a peon came in and gave a slip to Mrs. Kriplani. She looked up and asked Arjun to go to the Principal's office. Someone had to nudge him to go because he was reading a magazine under the desk. I noticed him going but didn't like think anything of it. Maybe he was going to get negative points for something. He's always getting negative points.

Just as class was ending, Arjun came running back in, looking like a crazy person. He was crying and his hair was all messed up and there was a peon running after him. And he ran straight at me! He was shouting. 'You crazy bitch!' he screamed. 'You crazy fucking bitch!' There was snot coming out his nose.

I couldn't even move I was so surprised. Thankfully I was sitting at the far end of the classroom (no one sits with me anymore) and some boys got hold of him before he could get to me. The peon came in running and started complaining loudly about how he had tried to hit the Principal and got into a fight with the peons in the Principal's office and had hit one of them with a chair and the peon was bleeding and stuff.

Anyway, the peon that had come with him stood very close to Arjun as he was getting his stuff together, throwing his books and things into his bag. The whole time he was crying and he looked awful, tears and snot running everywhere, swearing, using awful language, calling me all kinds of names, acting completely crazy.

At first I got mad. But then I saw how people were looking at him—with disgust. And how people were beginning to look at me. People were finally looking at me.

I didn't say anything. I was just glad that I'd blow-dried my hair that morning.

Rumours began to circulate that he had been expelled. Nobody knows why though there's tons of speculation. I figured he got caught doing drugs.

At Lunch today, three people smiled at me. And when I walked past my old gang, Nirav asked me what I thought had happened. I just smiled at him and said I didn't want to talk about it.

So I came home and I couldn't wait for Nusrat to be done washing dishes so I could tell her. And then—and THEN—the most unbelievable thing happened.

My mom came home from work early. And if that's not weird enough, she came into my room and shut the door and said, I need to talk to you.

I thought she was going to tell me that I had to apply to college in America. I was so sure she was going to tell me that she had called Wellesley and arranged things and that I would start there in the fall. My heart was beating so fast. I felt like I was in a cage.

She made me sit at my desk and then she sat on the bed but then she jumped up and began to pace up and down, up and down my room. At one point she picked up my old doll and then she walked up and down with the doll. It would have been funny if I hadn't been so scared.

Then she sat down again and...get this...she started crying! My mom! Crying! I had seen my mom cry once and that was when Sammy had broken his leg as a kid. That's it. I've never seen my mom cry. I've seen my dad cry millions of times but I've never seen my mom cry.

She put her face in her hands and just cried and cried and cried. 'I'm so sorry,' she kept saying. 'I'm so sorry, T.' It's been years since she called me that.

So here's the story: remember when I called Arjun over and did the bargain with him? About the six times? In the balcony? Well, I had forgotten that my parents room also opens out to the balcony because they never leave that door open. But that day she had. And she overheard. She heard everything. She heard the things I was willing to do, she heard him ask for them, she heard me say all the things I wanted him to take back, she heard him bargain.

And then she went to school and told the Principal. She forced the Principal to call Arjun to the office. I mean she didn't say that but I know my Principal and I know my mother and I'm telling you that's what happened. And when Arjun went to the office, my mom interrogated him in front of the Principal. Arjun is dumb as shit. He tried to lie but of course he didn't stand a chance with my mom.

She told the Principal that either she expels Arjun or my mom will file a case against Arjun and the school. But she said that the Principal might have expelled him anyway because there have been lots of other complaints.

She finished. Her head was in her hands and she was like sobbing. I was so stunned I didn't know what to say. I guess I was still thinking about the fact that my mom knew I had had sex. My mom knew the things everyone at school was saying about me. My mom knew the things I had promised to do for Arjun for those six times.

'Why didn't you tell me?' she asked.

I wanted to tell her that the thought of telling her hadn't even occurred to me. That I had thought of telling my father but that

I didn't think he would have been able to handle it. I wanted to tell her that if I had thought of telling her, I would have thought that she would have hit me.

I started crying. My mom pulled me into her arms and she cried some more. I smelled her around me, the starch in her sari, her perfume, her shampoo, the slight whiff of sweat from her armpits. I loved all of it.

My mom and I sat there and cried together for a long time. My mom looks beautiful when she cries. My mom is beautiful and I want to be beautiful like her. I told her that and she said that she is not beautiful all the time. I agreed with her in my head but I didn't say it.

My mom asked me if it had hurt with Arjun and I told her no. She asked me if I used protection and I was so glad I had. And Tanya, you know what, if it hadn't been for you and Nusrat, I wouldn't have. So thank you man. She started crying again and I told her it hadn't been bad at all. I told her he had been really sweet. I don't think she believed me.

It all seems so far away now, that night. I can't believe it happened. I know it had been good…it had right? But was it worth it? It would have been if he hadn't been such an asshole about it. I mean even if he had just broken up with me, I think I would have still not regretted it. But nothing was worth the last month. Nothing.

My mom asked me why being popular in school was so important to me. I asked her why working so hard at her job was so important to her. She pulled my nose and said that that is what paid for everything in our house. She was going to add that my father didn't make any money but I gave her a look and she didn't.

I told her that I felt like that was what I was good at. And then you know what she said? She said I was like light.

I'm like embarrassed to write it. My mom thinks I am like light. She said I am her light.

I mean I don't totally believe her now but I believed her then when she was saying it. I also totally got why my dad is still so in love with her. So fida over her. When my mom sets out to convince you about something, you want to get convinced. She's just like that.

We sat like that for a long time together. I heard the front door open and close and I knew that Nusrat had left. I wished she could have seen us like that. I wished she had a phone in her house so I could call her and tell her what had happened.

I wanted to ask my mom many things. I wanted to ask her why she and my dad were fighting so much. I wanted to ask her if she really thought I couldn't have a good life if I went to college in Bombay. I wanted to ask her if she loved Sammy more than me. I wanted to ask her if she and my dad would ever get a divorce.

In the end I didn't ask her anything. We just stayed like that until it got dark and then my mom got up to switch on the lights. If she hadn't done that, I would still be sitting there on my bed with her, in her lap, surrounded by her smell, surrounded by her sari, breathing in her hair and rubbing my cheek against her, feeling her heartbeat against mine, so steady, so sure.

I take back every mean thing I've ever said about my mother Tanya. Just take a black marker and erase all of them for me from my letters please? I never meant them. You knew that right?

Of course you did. You're super clever. And you don't get swayed by things stupid people say. You're super mature. You always knew I didn't mean any of that stuff. You always knew I love my mom. Did you know she loves me too? I wouldn't be surprised if you did. You're smarter than anyone I know except Nusrat. And you know what, Tanya Talati, I kind of love you.

Love,
Tania

*November 30, 1992*
*Karachi*

Dear Tania,

Wow, it sounds like everything has been sorted out in your life. How lovely for you.

I'm not surprised at your mother. I always thought you underestimated her. But please don't presume, based on your saccharine life, to understand mine. You don't know me, you don't know my mother, you don't know anything.

I thought I would let you know that my mother has finally decided to move back to America. I think that means she is going to divorce my father but I'm not sure as she hasn't said anything on that count.

They are selling the house. My mother said if he sells the house and gives her half the money she won't ask for any financial support ever again. So they're selling the house. The house I've lived in ever since we came back from America.

My father is going to buy a smaller house. Bibi will go with him. The last I heard, Chhoti Bibi has got a job in another house. I haven't seen her in a few days. She hasn't come to my room. I think she is done with her experiment of me.

My mother is going to go live in my grandparents' house in Boston. She is only taking clothes and photographs from here. Nothing else. Nothing else at all.

I called Navi to tell him all of this. He already knew. My father had called him and told him. I live in the same house as him and I had to hear his plans from my brother who is not in the same city. Navi plans to live with him and attend Aga Khan. He asked me what I was going to do. I told him I was going to go to college in America. He asked me what I will do if I don't get in. I don't know. Neither my father nor my mother have asked me that.

In case you are wondering, my mother has disappeared again. I don't go into her room anymore. I don't like to look at her anymore. I hate her tears. I hate the shape of her body under the covers.

I've sent off all my applications. Logically, I'd be surprised if I didn't get into at least one college. And the way things are now, no one will object even if I go to a safety school. All my father cares about is not having to pay.

I think it's time for us to stop this silly letter-writing. It seems we have come to a natural parting of ways. Let's not draw things out until they become awkward and painful.

I wish you the best of luck in your life, Tania. I hope your life continues to be happy and fortunate. And Nusrat. Please tell Nusrat that I wish her the best. That I have nothing but admiration for her.

Khuda Hafiz,
Tanya

~

*December 6, 1992*
*Bombay*

Dear Tanya,

Are you on crack? What's wrong with you? Why aren't you picking up the phone?

Look, I know you're depressed but you're being stupid. I know things are like really bad for you at home but why are you trying to break up with me?

Where's Ali? Did you fight with him? Did you break up with him too? What happened? I like Ali. I mean he's gay but I like him.

My parents are back to ignoring me mostly because they are fighting about this Hindutva stuff all the time. There are these things called Kar Sevaks and my mom says they're bad and my dad says what's wrong with having a little practice of Hinduism and then they begin to fight about that mosque and temple business. My mom hasn't said a word about college applications though so I think I'm staying in Bombay! Yay!

School is getting better. Did I tell you my big strategy? My big strategy is to act like nothing happened and like I don't care. It's not easy man. Stupid Soumya is acting like she's the new queen. As if a short little, fat little gremlin could ever replace me. But let her have her fun. Sooner or later, she's going to say something really stupid or do something really stupid or most likely, wear something really stupid and then that will be the end of her. I don't even have to do anything. I just have to wait for a repeat of her zebra crossing shirt with the tiger print tights.

Neenee has been pretty cool. For a while she didn't know what to do. Whether to ignore me along with everyone else or to like take advantage of the big hole in my social life and try to get more time with me. But now she hangs out with me and brings me gossip and tells me what everyone is saying. I think this whole fiasco has raised her social profile.

I'm focusing a lot on training the younger kids in sports. All sports. Soccer, basketball, gymnastics. Running. High jump. Long jump. It's actually been a lot of fun. I don't know whether they've heard the rumours about me or not but they don't seem to care. I mean they're kids, they'll run after any senior who gives them attention. And I am the girl Sports Captain of the school you know. There's this one kid Leila, she's great. She's so gutsy and she's really, really fast. And she picks things up really quickly. I wish she was in my house.

You know what's funny is that the Sports coach—the girls' Sports coach I mean—used to hate me. I mean like she would always find a reason to yell at me. So anyway, she's been seeing me spending time coaching the juniors and today she actually talked to me. Like not yelled at me. Talked to me. You know, about the girls. She also thinks Leila has a lot of potential.

I'm going to end this here because I want to post this quickly. I'll try you calling you again tonight.

Love,
Tania

~

*December 6, 1992*
*Bombay*

Dear Tanya,

Dude where are you? Things have gotten really bad and strange. I keep calling you but when someone finally picked up—I think it was Bibi—she said you weren't at home. And she hung up before I could ask for Chhoti Bibi. Dude I hope you're okay.

So first of all, they broke down that mosque today. It was all over the news. It was horrible Tanya. I mean I don't care about any of this stuff but it was horrible watching it on TV. All these people all wearing orange like a huge human wave on the wall and then all over the mosque. It's huge that mosque. It looks like a temple.

And our policemen? Just standing there doing nothing. I mean what were they there for?

And now everyone seems really worried and there's a very weird feeling all around. As if something is going to happen. But what more can happen right? The mosque has already been destroyed. Do you know it was from the 15th century? What assholes! How can you do that! I mean people barely live one hundred years and this mosque has been there for over four hundred years. It wasn't cool man.

I also got really mad at my dad because obviously my mom was totally right and he was totally like STUPID to not see the signs.

Anyway, they sent us all home from school early. My dad came and picked me up and he looked so sad and so worried I didn't say a word to him. Of course he had NOT known that the Hindutva people were going to do this. He had believed them when they had said that the kar sevaks were just going to do puja and stuff. Puja is a good thing. Puja is not breaking things. My father hadn't known what these guys were going to do. How could he have known? He did not know.

Anyway so he took me home and we dropped Jenny home along the way. Well, Jenny couldn't go home actually because she lives in Dadar so she went home to her friend Aanchal's house. I don't know them really well, they're not in my group. Well, my old group. But I saw them standing outside the school looking lost and it seems that the school bus wasn't working so they didn't know what to do. My dad dropped them home to Aanchal's house. Aanchal lives in a house not a building. It's in a weird part of town I haven't seen before. But they were super nice and said thank you many times to my dad. My dad barely noticed he looked so sad and upset. He waited though till they went upstairs and waved from the balcony.

When we got home, Nusrat was there. Her school was also let out early and apparently the road to her house has been closed so she came here.

But Tanya, Nusrat is acting weird. I don't get it. She's not talking to me. She's super worried about her parents and so my mom called them and spoke to them and Nusrat got on the phone and just started crying—her crying you know—where she makes those sounds. And I felt so bad I went to give her a hug from behind and Tanya she just like flung me off! It was so weird! It was like she didn't want me to touch her.

My dad saw that I was feeling bad and she whispered to me that Nusrat is really worried and that I shouldn't feel bad. I mean hello I am her best friend of course I know she is totally worried you don't need to tell ME!

Anyway, I'm going to post this letter now so that hopefully you get it soon. Maybe you didn't get my last letter. I don't know. But it's really scary to not hear from you while all this shit is going on. Please write. Give me a blank call and I'll call you back. I'm going to try you again tonight.

Love,
Tania

PS: Just saw on the news—150 people have been killed. My mom says it's going to get a lot worse before it gets better.

~

*December 8, 1992*
*Bombay*

Listen dude I don't know what your problem is but you're being a real asshole. I have called you like a zillion times and I know that you know because one time Chhoti Bibi picked up and I could hear her calling you and I could hear her telling you to come talk to me.

I don't get it. What happened? Did I do something? Did I say something bad and like insensitive? Come on Tanya you know I didn't mean it. Please call me.

Nusrat is still being weird and Bombay is burning. You can see the smoke from our balcony in so many different directions and every day it feels like there it is coming from a new direction.

The names of places don't seem to matter anymore as names of places but only in saying whether Muslims live there or Hindus. And the funny thing about Bombay is that there is no one place where it's all Hindus or all Muslims, at least not in the poor places. Except the Jain and Marwari buildings. I guess you can do anything when you have money. It is like SO important to be rich.

Although nothing is sacred right now, not enough money. Even in our building we have taken down all the name plates of all houses so that if the mobs come they won't know where the Muslims live. And dude Tanya, our building is one of the nicest in the city. If the mobs really come here then they can go anywhere.

Names on TV: Ghatkopar, Bhandup, Jogeshwari. Dadar, Matunga, Mahim, Tardeo. Deonar, Pydhonie, Dongri. Dadar, Byculla, Mohammed Ali Road, Bombay Central. Dadar is where Jenny lives. Byculla is where Aniza Khumri lives. Bombay Central is where we go to buy fish at Crawford Market. Mahim is near the beach. Matunga is where our driver lives.

Nusrat lives in Bhendi Bazaar. She lives in a chawl. Do you know what a chawl is? It's like a really old building with a long narrow balcony where people string out all their clothes to dry. And they live like ten people to a room and then they have to share a bathroom with other rooms that also have many many people. But even these rooms cost thousands and thousands of rupees because Bombay is like really expensive.

Nusrat is being really weird. I mean I get that she's really worried about her dad because he's super hot-headed and you know there are Muslim gangs as well right now going around trying to kill Hindus. The more you hear about the Muslim gangs, the more orange flags and the more columns of smoke I can see from my window.

On TV and in newspapers, there is a scary political party saying the worst kinds of things. They want to kill Muslims. They want to kill people from other states. They want to kill people who are not born here. They want to kill a lot of people.

Isn't it weird that I, Tania Ghosh, am sitting here writing you this letter and I am using the word 'kill'? I mean when did that happen? When did normal people like you and me begin to talk about killing as if we're talking about clothes or cricket or a new restaurant? You know what I mean? Like it's not supposed to be in our vocabulary. Not normal people.

So anyway I get that Nusrat is really worried about her dad and she has been crying a lot but sometimes she looks at me and I feel…this is so weird but I feel like she is crying about me, not her dad. But she won't like talk to me it's so weird. She made a huge fuss when my mom told her to sleep in my room. I mean we used to love it when she stayed to help at parties and spent the night in my room. I thought maybe it was because she was suddenly feeling touchy about sleeping on the mattress on the floor but when I told her to sleep on my bed she just looked at me like I'd slapped her and tried to say no. And Nusrat trying to say anything is really horrible. So I just said okay, okay, you don't have to.

She won't watch TV with me, we're not allowed out of the house, she will barely stay in my room. She really, really wants to go home because she's convinced that her father will run off to join the gangs. But my parents won't let her leave the house. And at least they haven't said Bhendi Bazaar on TV yet.

You know I never really thought about who is Muslim in my class until now. And I had to sit down and write out all the names and then show it to my parents and ask them. I don't see any rhyme or reason to it and don't know how they can tell. Sometimes a wala is a Bori and sometimes it's a Parsi. Sometimes a Dalal is Hindu and sometimes it's Muslim. How do you know?

And how come there is an Ayesha Parekh when we all know that Ayesha is a Muslim name and Parekh is a Hindu surname?

Why doesn't it make any sense? Why has no one taught us this in school? I mean isn't this more important to learn especially if no one takes the Constitution seriously and goes around doing random morchas and killing people? I mean what is up with that?

My mom is acting like all of this is my dad's fault. She's so crazy sometimes. I mean he picked the wrong side but obviously it was a mistake.

There are nine Muslims in my class of forty. I called all of them even Mustafa Habibwala who I haven't said one word to since we were four years old in Nursery School and he bit me on my bottom. They are all fine. Anizaa Khumri sounded really surprised to hear from me and also, really scared. She told me she lives in Byculla. As soon as she said it I knew it was bad because I was hearing Byculla on the TV all the time, more than the other names. She actually started crying on the phone. Said they were locked into the house from the outside and her grandmother was going to die because she needs dialysis. I wanted to tell her to come to my house but that's the thing with riots no one can go anywhere. It's the worst feeling in the world to sit in your house and watch crazy, angry people on the TV doing things, doing horrible things all with torches and swords and huge sticks and broken bottles of glass and their eyes are all mad and you know it's not far away. And then you go stand at the window of the opposite side of the house, the window that doesn't look out on the city and there's the sea. And the sea doesn't know because the sea is just the same as it is every day, grey with white foam, coming in every few minutes to crash like a crazy person on the rocks and die. Over and over again. And if you watch the waves long enough you begin to forget the other window and everything outside it. And you begin to feel like a little bit better like a little bit normal and your brain even begins to think about what's on

TV tonight and then you suddenly notice that no one is down there, no one is down by the rocks and you remember everything and it's not a bad dream.

There's no one by the sea. No one. Not even the lovers who are always there. Not even the children from the government building nearby throwing bags of rubbish into the sea. Not even the poor people who go there to shit in the dark so people can't see their bums.

Where are they going now?

~

*December 8, 1992*
*Bombay*

Dear Tanya,

No one is allowed to leave the building. There are lots of police outside. Things have become really, really bad dude. Like really bad.

My parents keep watch on the TV so that one of them is always watching it. They throw us out of the room when bad stuff comes on. I wish they wouldn't do that. The stuff in my head has got to be a lot worse than what they are showing. It's got to be because it's really bad.

Nusrat has completely lost it. They said Bhendi Bazaar is engulfed in fire.

It happened this morning. She has just lost it. She ran to the front door as they were saying it but my dad grabbed her and pulled her back. It was so awful Tanya. The way she was crying the way she's not even able to speak. Just those horrible, horrible sounds that seem like they're coming from the pit of her stomach. She collapsed on my dad and just cried and cried and cried. My parents gave her something that made her sleep.

We haven't been able to get through to her parents. I've been calling every ten minutes.

Things are really bad. They're stripping men to see if they're Hindu or Muslim.

Many houses have lost electricity and water. Everyone is telling everyone else to stay calm and not believe rumours. I mean if they don't want people to believe rumours they shouldn't have the news show all this stuff. Because they say different numbers every time. Sometimes it's 30 people in Nalla Nagar and sometimes it's 200. Sometimes it's Byculla and sometimes it's not. But Tanya Bhendi Bazaar is one of the worst hit areas. It's like really bad.

I'm so scared. I'm so scared of what will happen to Nusrat if something has happened to her parents. Her parents are her life. How will she live with it?

I hate watching her sleep with whatever my parents gave her. She looks dead. But I'm even more scared of what will happen when she wakes up.

God please take care of Nusrat God please take care of Nusrat. Tanya you pray too. You pray Muslim prayers. Who knows who is listening. Tell Chhoti Bibi too.

Love,
Tania

~

*December 9, 1992*
*Bombay*

Dear Tanya,

I am writing this letter to you so that you know everything. Nusrat left. We woke up in the morning and she wasn't there, the shorts and t-shirt she had borrowed from me were folded neatly on the mattress on my floor. Her school uniform is gone.

My parents have called the police and given them a description but there are so many missing people right now. Missing women missing men missing children. I don't think the police are even going to look even though my mom took the phone from my dad and said a lot of stuff about who she knows and how much influence she has.

The police are not going to do anything.

I haven't told my parents this but Nusrat left a note in my wallet. It says:

Dear Tania,

I have taken five hundred rupees. I'm sorry I thought we were best friends. I can see now that you were just being kind. I will always love you. Always have. Always will.

Yours always, Nusrat.

I don't understand. What is she talking about? We are best friends. Why does it sound like a farewell letter? Is she trying to break up with me? Why does everyone keep breaking up with me?

It is the middle of the afternoon and my mother is taking a nap. My father has fallen asleep in front of the TV. The news is on.

Tanya, I am going to go look for Nusrat. I have to.

I don't know whether you knew this was going to happen and if that is why your last letter was like a farewell letter. I mean it would be damn weird if you knew because no one knew the riots were going to happen although many people on TV are saying the government knew but that doesn't make sense because what government would want their richest city to burn like this day after day?

I can't not go Tanya. The smoke from the window is now from all directions and even if I go to the other window and look at the sea, I can't forget, not even for a minute.

So I have to go.

I hope you understand. I hope you're okay. I will call you when I come back.

Love,
Tania

# 12

May 29, 1996
Columbia, MA

Dear Tania,

Graduation was yesterday. It went well. I got a prize established by an old, dead Indian alumnus for the student from South Asia with the highest GPA. You know, if my father hadn't changed my passport from American to Pakistani so many years ago, I wouldn't have been able to get the award. I graduated summa cum laude. Less than 5% of a class of 1300.

I'm graduating from college at the top of my class and I have a job at the world's biggest investment banking firm with a salary I cannot even imagine being able to spend. I have friends. Real friends. They know me and have stayed friends. Actually we've grown closer since freshman year. Some of them are moving to the city with me. I've had two boyfriends in the last four years and several flings. I still haven't enjoyed sex but I plan to. I've been going to a psychiatrist for four years and each year they held the payment of my scholarship until she certified that I am not a suicide risk.

I have written you thirteen letters. This is my last letter to you.

You must know by now everything that happened. I know you know. But somehow, since this is the last letter, I want to say it to *you, face to face, it was me. Of course it was me. I wrote Nusrat that letter. I'm sorry. I'm sorry. I'm sorry.*

*I know I have no excuse. And you know I'm sorry. I know you know. I also know it's not enough. I know it will never, ever be enough. Nothing will.*

*In my last letter to you from Karachi, I had said that you couldn't understand. You didn't understand, Tania, that part was true. You with your volatile, passionate family, your mother who stood up to your bully of a boyfriend, your father who was soft and sweet. And Nusrat with you by the sea, her hand in yours. Always there.*

*But what I have learnt is that maybe you could have learned to understand. Maybe I was in no position to explain but just because you didn't understand didn't mean you couldn't understand. I've realized that. Look at me. I am not even from Bombay, I wasn't there in December 1992 and yet, it did happen to me. Because of you, it happened to me. Maybe you would have understood, then, how completely alone in the world I felt in those terrible days when my parents were splitting up and Navi couldn't come home and no one had even thought to ask what would happen to me. No one asked, Tania. Not even my mother. I never came first with anyone. But in those terrible days, I became invisible.*

*I don't know why I never said anything. No amount of therapy will ever explain to me why I never asked my mother when she decided to go to America, what about me? Will you leave me behind if I don't get a scholarship to a college in America? I never asked her that. I also never asked my father about a fixed deposit I found in his office with a note tacked on it that said 'Navi college fees'. I never asked him, where's Tanya's? Where IS Tanya? I never asked. I have always been mute with my family.*

*I've bought the tickets for my mother and me to go to India this summer. Right before I start work. I'm going to go on my way to Pakistan. Yes, that's right. I'm going to go back to Pakistan for the first time since I left. My father asked me to come.*

*Yes, imagine that.*

*He was here for graduation. I'm sure Navi forced him to come. He looked so much older, so much thinner, he reminded me instantly of my mother. He looked ill at ease and kept complaining about America. The weather is too cold, the people are too fat, the food is too bland. I think the only time he was silent was when I took them to our library. I should say one of our libraries because Columbia has several. But I took him to the one that I use, the one I study at, the one I've worked at throughout my four years here. My father sat down suddenly on a bench and was silent. I sat down next to him and said nothing.*

*'You went to college here,' he said. I nodded.*

*'I had forgotten that it is like this over here. In America.'*

*He sounded sorrowful.*

*'You will never come back home.'*

*I wanted to ask him if he wanted me to come back to Pakistan. I said nothing. It was the first time in many years that I had sat with my father at all.*

*He talked about his life in Karachi. The hospital which was now functional in two wings. He had started a clinic in a slum.*

*'Chhoti Bibi started me on it.'*

*Chhoti Bibi now runs my father's house. I guess she made her dream come true.*

*Then he said it had been four years since I had come back to Pakistan. That it was time I came home. I wanted to tell him that it wasn't home for me anymore, hadn't been since he had let me go without a word. But I am not you. I am still not you.*

*I will never be you. Did you even realize how much I had wanted to? And I still can't fully fathom why. We had no dream in common, no ambition in common and no doubt, we still would not. You were as insecure as I had been and with as few real relationships. Except for your mother. And father. And Nusrat.*

*'Tania, I want you to know that I didn't get your last few letters until much, much afterwards. I didn't know what was going to*

*happen. How would I know? Do you know when the Karachi newspapers started covering the Bombay riots? Only from December 6. And it was all about Babri Masjid. All about Ram Janmbhoomi. All about Ayodhya. I couldn't have known that what was happening in Ayodhya was going to come to Bombay. I couldn't have known, Tania. And I never got those last letters from you before the riots. I didn't know it was coming. I had no way of knowing.*

*It is six in the evening, going on seven and there is still light outside, it is as if it's the middle of the day. That's the wonder of this country. One month ago, this bench had snow in it and the tree overhead had no leaves. And now it is warm and the leaves are bursting over each other in baby newness, the lightest of greens, poking everywhere, wildly, ferociously and in complete abandon. I am sitting here writing this to you, the buildings stretching out into the distance, still fulfilling a promise they made me the first time I came here as a freshman. To be here, to always be here.*

*I must go. A friend is driving me to my new apartment in Battery Park City. I am going to go spend the first night in my brand new apartment. In a sleeping bag but oh the bathroom has marble tiles and the doorman downstairs wears white gloves.*

*There's my friend again. He has called my name twice now. Tanya. Tania.*

*I will never stop being sorry. But I am going to live my life now like I know you're living yours. Your mother sent a picture to my mother. The four of you on a beach somewhere with Sammy's Nigerian girlfriend. You are impossibly beautiful. You're looking straight into the camera, straight at me. I cut out the picture and have it with me. I used to look at it every day before going to sleep. I'd like to stop doing that now.*

*I hope you will always be brave and always call bullshit on everything that doesn't make sense to you. If there is one gift I can give you it is to say that if it gets too big and too painful, you can let it go. You can always let it go because I will never, ever set it down.*

*It is like another heart that I carry, one that never beats but is there next to mine. I will carry it with me till the day I die.*

*I hope you forgive me one day. But even if you don't, I will always carry it with me. I hope that knowing that, knowing the truth of it, knowing that it happened to both of us, you can set it down sometimes, when it gets too heavy, when it gets too hard. I hope knowing that I will always carry it will bring you just a little bit of peace.*

*Khuda Hafiz,*
*Tanya*

~

November 21, 1992
*Karachi*

Dear Nusrat,

It is strange to write to you as we have never spoken nor written to each other before. However, woman to woman, I owe you this.

Tania just called me. We talked for a long time. Much of what we talked about has nothing to do with you or things that you will understand. But we did spend a little time talking about you and that is why I am now writing to you.

Before I go into the point of this letter, let me tell you why I'm writing it at all. The truth is, Nusrat, I've always felt an affinity with you. Always felt that in a different world, we could have been friends. Real friends, not play-acting in a childish fantasy as you have been with Tania. Real friends. Equal friends.

I really admire your grit, Nusrat. Your tenacity, your obvious intelligence and ambition. I'd like to think we have these qualities in common. Although, of course, I fully recognise that given the adversity you face and will always face, your achievements far outstrip mine, as Tania had once pointed out. She has a lot of admiration for you. You should believe that because it is true.

You seem to me to have a lot of dignity. A lot of self-esteem. I do too. I thought about it for a long time and I think if I had been you, I would have wanted to know.

Nusrat, Tania doesn't think of you the way you think of her. She is fond of you, don't get me wrong. But she is worried that you think more of your friendship than she does. That you have perhaps *misinterpreted* her kindness to you. That time when her mother was angry about her not applying to American colleges and you threw yourself at her. That was embarrassing for her, Nusrat. She feels uncomfortable when you hug her. She doesn't know how to tell you. She's too soft-hearted. You know Tania.

She said she wants you to make more friends of your own so she can spend time with her friends. She has to make new friends now that she's going to college. Friends she can go to real places with. Public places.

Of course she's fond of you. She's very fond of you. You must never doubt that.

I also told her that I'm sure you do have friends to go back to and that she shouldn't worry about you. I feel like I would have wanted that said about me if I had been you. Keep your pride. Keep your dignity.

I hope I haven't overstepped my bounds in writing to you. I hope you understand the very good intentions this letter comes from. After all, we both want what's best for Tania.

I'm probably going to come visit her soon before I leave for college in America. It would be lovely to meet. Are you sure you are not interested in studying abroad? You have a compelling profile. If I can offer any guidance or advice, please don't ever hesitate to ask. I'd be so happy to help you.

With warm wishes,
Tanya

# 13

Nusrat has been gone for six hours and thirty seven minutes when you leave to look for her. Your parents were united in their refusal to take you even though you cried and begged. The curfew was absolute, they said. They told you that the police were shooting on sight. That everything had broken down and that nothing could be done. You had screamed at them, what is the point of being rich then? And they had looked back at you with infinite pity in their eyes.

You slip out of the house in the middle of the afternoon, leaving the door ajar so the sound of it closing wouldn't wake them from their nap. There is one moment of paralysis when you imagine people entering your house through that open door, the mobs coming in to kill them in your absence. But the yellow lift doors open as they always do. You get in because you have to find Nusrat.

Downstairs a soft breeze comes in from the sea and for a moment you are tempted to run to it to see if she is on the rocks there, just waiting for you with a big smile and fanciful comments in her notebook for you to read. You are wearing her salwar kameez and now you wrap her dupatta around your head so that her scent surrounds you, her stubborn smile almost real in front of you, her bangles clinking against your hand.

Everything is silent downstairs. There is no napping watchman, no drivers wiping down cars, no maids chatting in a circle under the banyan tree, no children playing in the garden. There is only a mountain of garbage piled up in the corner, black with flies. A surfeit of dead leaves blows restlessly across the grounds. You are suddenly and acutely aware that no one knows that you are outside. You badly want to turn back and go home but you don't because you have to find Nusrat.

You can't leave through the gate where five policemen stand in bulletproof vests unzipped in the heat. There are long, thin guns resting next to their plastic chairs. The guns make you recoil, you Bombay girl who has never seen them. You turn around and leave your building through a secret hole that children use to go out to the candy man, five sweets for a rupee and one extra sometimes if you smile just so and say please.

No one sees you leave.

You run quickly down the road in case your mother wakes up and looks out the window. There are very few cars on the road. You remember your childhood desire to lie down in the middle of the road and watch the gulls swoop above and think that today, if you had time, you could do that. Today if you lie down right before the traffic light, in front of Sun restaurant and Croissants Café, no car would come and find you there, spread-eagled right on the big white arrow that points, of its own accord, to the sea.

You know the way to Bhendi Bazaar because you had looked it up on a Western India Automobile Association map your father keeps in a drawer with the car keys. You have it with you, drawn out on a piece of paper with the landmarks you know. Breach Candy hospital, Noor Mohammed's furniture store, the shop with the sev puri, the Jain temple, Cadbury House, Heera Panna with its smuggled shampoos and then straight on from there towards Tardeo and Byculla where your knowledge of landmarks ends. All you know of Nusrat's house is that it is in a crowded street in an old chawl with petticoats and underwear hanging from every window. On the ground floor of the chawl is a crowded bakery whose wiry team of teenage boys had impressed you the one time you had dropped Nusrat home in your car. You remember stopping the car to stare at them. How quickly they took orders and how quickly they dispensed soft buns of bread in tiny brown paper packages tied up with the same brown string that Nusrat had wrapped up her certificates in.

Bombay is become a city for ghosts and you don't recognise it. The roads are wide with no cars, the pavements loom empty with no street vendors, no gaggle of beggar children, no balloon seller, no crazy woman hitting her forehead and haranguing the world. Only the crows and gulls and vultures cry out, much closer to the ground than usual surely because their shadows graze your skin.

You can't shake the feeling that people are watching you even though all the windows are closed and in the old buildings, the cracked blue and green shutters are boarded up. You walk fast, looking at no one because you have to find Nusrat.

You smell Noor Mohammed's furniture store before you see it. When you reach it, the gaping black emptiness is incomprehensible, the stench of burnt furniture makes you stumble. You reach out to steady yourself and your hand falls on the remains of a glass-fronted cabinet you had made fun of with Neenee only a week ago, laughing at the gaudy gold inlays and wishing it into each other's wedding trousseaus. It is lying on its side now, half of it gone, the gold edges black with soot. You wish now that you hadn't made fun of it. You wish, absurdly, to go back and put your arms around the shiny gold cabinet and say to it that you're so sorry for making fun of it, that you would have loved to have it in your house.

You start to run. The carcasses of the burnt furniture seem alive and you can't bear to see the legs of chairs stick out into the pavement, as if trying to escape their burnt bodies.

There are police huddled in jeeps at some intersections. You stay away from them, running in the shadows of tall buildings. They stay away from you too, sitting in their cars, not seeing you in Nusrat's salwar kameez, servant girl, invisible.

The traffic lights go from green to yellow to red and then back to green but there are no cars to stop and no cars to go. If Nusrat was with you, she would have understood the lump this brings to your throat. The solitude of your witness oppresses you.

You walk and run and walk and run. Sweat runs freely down your back and you wish you had thought to bring along water. You wish you had thought to bring along many things that occurred to you only now that you were on the streets—water, money, a knife, a stick, a torch.

It had not seemed so far on the map.

You come to a market. There are now more policemen and more police jeeps. You heard the crackle of their wireless sets as you walked by, indecipherable shouting and crackle but the policemen stand glued, watching each other with anxious eyes. You hear the words 'Muslim' and 'Hindu' and 'dargah' and 'masjid' several times. You hear 'aag lag gaya' once, a high-pitched shriek that make the men stamp their legs uneasily like horses. But they stay where they are and they don't see you. You keep going because you have to find Nusrat.

The streets narrow and become dirty. Garbage is strewn everywhere. You see a dead crow, its head and beak absurdly intact while rats nibble on dark red entrails.

All the shops are boarded up and the boards are full of smiling actors and cricketers holding batteries, biscuits and Bournvita. Where there are no boards, there is tarpaulin tacked tightly across windows and doors and you wonder absently why tarpaulin is always blue and decide that it must be to keep away mosquitoes although you can't remember why you think that. You think that Nusrat will know and you remind yourself to ask her when you find her.

The road becomes a street and the street becomes narrow with barely enough room for two people to walk side by side. But you can feel people. Behind barricaded doors. Behind barred windows. Somewhere a baby cries.

You feel like things are touching you, people are touching you. At first, every noise makes you run but you are tired now. When someone coughs so close to you, it feels like it must be a spirit in your head; you steel yourself to not run and you continue to walk, endlessly, pretending not to hear the baby whose weeping follows you.

The silence feels slick to you. It takes energy to not imagine your father coming to get you (and in your daydream he comes for you in a little white Maruti he used to have but had sold a long time ago) and you give up trying to hold the fantasy at bay. You think so long as you keep going it's okay to imagine him coming to get you. So long as you keep going to find Nusrat. So long as you find Nusrat.

You want to call her name but will they think you are Muslim and what if that is a bad thing? Or what if they think you are looking for her because she's Muslim? Better to stay silent.

It is when you get to the end of the galli that the smell hits you so that before you know it, you're bent over double and vomiting, your torso bent forward because even in the act of vomiting you remember not to get it on your new Reebok shoes.

Later on, when you remember that moment, you can't understand how it is that you knew what the smell was but you did. You even thought you were prepared for it when you turned the corner.

What hits you the most is how casually they are dead. One is sitting on a step outside a house, leaning against a pillar that is red with blood from a hole in the side of his head where flies buzz. The rest of him is untouched in blue and white shorts.

Two other men lie together, with blood pooled between their chests and one man's leg flung over the other as if they had died in an illicit embrace.

You walk away slowly, trying not to step on anything, trying not to hear the pitter patter of blood dripping from their bodies into muddy pools of water where the road had been potholed by the rain several years ago and had never been filled.

Nusrat. You have to find to find Nusrat.

There is a sound in the background. Like a continuous breeze rustling. Like the sound of waves. Like very, very soft music. You have been ignoring it for some time but it is growing louder and it no longer sounds like the sea or the wind or music.

The absolute silence around you suddenly makes sense, why there was no grieving wife or mother prostrate over the bodies of the dead men. It is the silence of fear. Somewhere there is a sea of angry men, crazy men, coming down the road towards you. You realise, with a sudden, sick certainty, that this is why everything is hidden, this is why everyone is indoors.

You see a shop that has no door anymore. A tiny stall of a shop that used to sell light bulbs and wires and switches and extension cords. Torn Diwali lights hang from the ceiling but almost everything else has been taken, the shelves are bare and broken glass lies everywhere. There is a crunch of glass and a dog appears. You look at the dog and the dog looks at you. You enter the shop and the dog enters behind you. The counter is miraculously still standing and you think about hiding behind the counter. You make a space and crouch in the corner and the dog comes and sits next to you, both of you hidden from the street by the counter of the shop which has no goods for sale in its display cases. The dog is staring at you without blinking. You hold out a hand but he doesn't move. He sits next to you, watching you, measuring you. In a shard of mirror you see yourself on the floor and for a moment you think you have found Nusrat.

There is suddenly noise outside. Sounds of running footsteps. A man shouts once, twice, 'Samir!'

There is a banging of a door and then there is silence.

The sound of the crowd is becoming louder and louder. It is the voices of people, all raised, all shouting, an indistinguishable protest that wafts down the silent street to you as if it is a smell. The dog gets up and leaves.

You wish for obstacles to put between you and the coming men. You wish you had taken boxes and crates from the street and put them in front of you. Anyone who looks into the shop, anyone who peers over the counter will you see hiding in the corner. Your heart is beating so loudly that you think people in the street will be able to hear it and you clasp both your hands over it. Your body is burning, you have fever and any moment your father's hand will descend with a cool wet cloth on your forehead and you will be in bed at home, cold from the cloth, hot from the fever.

The sound of the crowd is coming closer and closer, it grows louder and louder. Your father doesn't come, your fever doesn't go. Your body catches fire and turns electric.

You can make out words now.

A roar: 'Jai Bhavani Jai Shivaji!'

A roar: 'Pakistan ya kabristan!'

A roar: 'Shiv Sena Zindabad!'

A roar: 'Haath mein lungi, mooh mein paan, bhago laundya Pakistan!'

Your world has shrunk to the gap between the counter and the wall of the shop whose broken glass reflects pieces of the street. You hope they can't see you the way you can see the hazy reflection of a bobbing wave of men marching down the street, two by two, two by two, two by two.

You can smell them now. Sweat and alcohol and rotting garbage. They are marching past the electrical shop. You think about what you will do if they find you. If they will take off your clothes and hurt you. You admit to yourself that if you had known, you would not have come, not even for Nusrat. Yet now here you are lying on the floor of an electrical shop, the kind of shop that would never supply bulbs and sockets to your beautiful house with its chandelier from France and sweet, fake lanterns from a beach in Goa. A small shop, a small shop in a crowded market lane you could never have imagined going to and yet here you are lying on the floor, taking shelter in its walls, worrying that they will find you, worrying that they will drag you out and do things to you. You see yourself dead, draped over the counter of the shop and you hope that if that happens, someone will call your mother and not your father.

The crowd outside is restive. Someone says there are none left. Someone else says that the motherfuckers have gone to Pakistan. Another man is shouting, rundi, rundi, rundi. You remember the word written in English in the corner of your notebook when you had left it on your desk over Lunch Break. Slut.

'Chal Azhar ki galli!'

A cheer goes up. Someone abuses Azhar and his mother and grandmother and father and daughter. Someone imagines how he will look without a penis. The men laugh and step loudly, as if the ground is slipping beneath them. The slap slap of sandals and shoes is loud in your ears and then slowly begin to recede.

Silence.

It takes you a long time to get up. You are surprised by how much your left leg has bled where a piece of glass is sticking deep into your calf. You pull it out and the pain makes the world spin.

You take your teeth to the bottom of your kameez and tear a hole and then a strip that you tie around the wound. You can't bring yourself to take Nusrat's dupatta off your head.

You stumble through many silent streets. Everywhere the windows are boarded up and everywhere there is stink of garbage that made you want to vomit over and over again but there is nothing left. Your throat is burning and you stop at a house and bang on the door to ask for water. You hear people inside but no one opens the door. The sun is shining brightly and your head hurts. Images are beginning to swim in front of your head and you know you need to get to water fast.

And then you see a building with a shop on the ground floor that is completely burnt. No sign, no counter, nothing except for a naked old man lying across the threshold of the shop, looking, except for the way his legs are bent, as if he is peacefully asleep. You turn your face away from his genitals, like softly spreading wax between his legs.

It's the bakery from Nusrat's chawl. You look up and it doesn't look like the same building with all the windows boarded up. Where are the petticoats hanging outside windows? Where is the underwear with holes?

You stop at the small doorway of the building and wrap your dupatta around your face so only your eyes are visible. You wish for your father again. You wish for a torch. You wish you had eaten carrots so you could see better in the dark. But you climb up the steps and into the dark.

You hear keening.

You want to run away but you grip the wall, palms pushing into cold stone, and you slide inside slowly. The dark is a monster and you, who have never been afraid of the dark, are terrified.

The keening gets louder and it's behind a closed door. You knock on it softly but it can't be heard. You bang on it, the dark is closing in on you.

The keening stops and someone comes to the door. You can hear them and you imagine them scared, you imagine them wrapping their dupatta around and you wonder why it is that women cover themselves with flimsy cloth when they are scared as if cloth ever stopped anyone and you know it doesn't because it never stopped Arjun but you are doing it too and so there you are, you and the woman behind the door who has stopped keening and both of you have dupattas wrapped around your head as if it will save you from each other.

The door opens a crack and a shadow of a face shows. She asks you in Hindi who you are. You say Tania because you can't think of anything else and as soon as you say it you wonder if you should have said a more Hindu name or a more Muslim name and how did they know to kill the guy with the right side of his head chopped off had they asked him his name?

The woman is silent and you whisper that you are looking for Nusrat. The woman shakes her head and shuts the door and won't open it even though you knock loudly, urgently, continuously.

She opens the door again and she looks tired. 'Please go away,' she says.

'It's my friend,' you say. 'Please Aunty.'

'Friend!' she looks at you. 'My husband is missing and you're looking for a friend!'

'Sister!' you shout, holding the door open with your hand. 'My sister! Please Aunty please! I've been looking for her for so long!'

The exhaustion and the heat and the buzzing in your head all come together and you can't bear it anymore and you sag against the wall. The corridor sways and recedes, sways and recedes.

The woman makes an exclamation of disgust, looks both ways into the dark corridor and pulls you into her house.

Inside it's dark and it smells bad except for two incense sticks that burn in front of a picture of a fair man in a white cap with a gold border that you've seen at your Bohra friends' houses.

She pushes you at a mat on the floor and disappears. You discover the warm, fast breathing bodies of two very small children on the mattress, one a baby.

She comes back with a steel tumbler of water and you can't help but remember everything your mother had ever said about drinking water outside your house but you can't help it, you take the tumbler and drain it at one go.

'Now go,' says the woman, taking the tumbler. 'Please leave. I don't want any trouble.'

'Nusrat Mohammedbhai,' you say. 'Her father is a carpenter. She is mute.'

'I don't know.'

But she says it too quickly and you don't believe her. You grab her hand. 'Please Aunty please, she really is my sister. Please tell me. I know she lives in this building but I don't know which floor.'

She shakes off your hand and begins to cry.

Why is she crying? What does it mean?

'I hate them!' she says. 'I hate all of them. It's to protect them that my husband went.'

'Protect Nusrat?'

'Protect the women of the building. My husband and two other men took all the women to the mosque in the next neighbourhood. They left six hours ago when the trouble started in the morning and they haven't come back yet.'

Her voice broke on the last words and she started crying, softly, still very softly, muted into her dupatta, as if it was dangerous to be scared, dangerous to be sad.

'You're sure Nusrat was with him?'

She suddenly looks at you with hatred in her eyes.

'Bhaarh mein jaaye teri Nusrat! Bhaar mein jaaye!'

You oddly want to comfort her, to put your arm around her. One of the children's sleeping arms falls on your lap and you almost scream.

She picks him up and you see that it is a baby. He is peeing in his sleep.

'I've drugged him,' she says, her voice quavering. 'I've drugged him so he won't cry. I wouldn't let them take him. But he hasn't woken up since morning, not once.'

She holds him close and her face disappears in the curve of the sleeping boy, his arms hanging slackly over her shoulder. There is something disturbing about his deep sleep. You wish you could pick him up and take him home so he would wake up among the gay mosaic tile in the kitchen where he would crouch on his baby haunches, picking at the margins.

'Please tell me where they went.'

She looks at you suspiciously. 'Why? Who are you? Nusrat has no sister.' She looks at your shoes which shine white in the darkness.

'I'm her friend from school.'

'What's your surname?'

'Sheikh. Tania Sheikh.'

'Where do you live?'

'Colaba.'

She is silent, disbelieving.

'I have come with my father in his car to take her back home with me. She is my second cousin. My father's brother's daughter. Cousin.'

'Salim Mohammedbhai's brother?'

You nod.

'Salim Bhai has rich relatives,' she says finally. 'If only he wasn't so hot-headed he wouldn't be poor and here with us.'

'Where did they go, Aunty?'

'To Momin Masjid,' she says finally. 'Near the big Catholic school.'

You jump up. You know the school. You had passed it on the way. It is cream and green with a fake Christmas tree right inside the gate and a giant sign in popsicle sticks saying MERRY CHRISTMAS although half the T has fallen off.

'You should not go.'

'Come with me.'

Her eyes light up which you suddenly notice are beautiful, a soft brown with vivid edges. But then she shakes her head and tightens her arm around the comatose baby.

You get up to leave and she grabs your arm. 'Find my husband! Please, find my husband! I will do anything for you, just find my husband!'

To your shock, she falls to the floor, the baby still in her arms, and tries to touch your Reebok shoes. You say, 'No, no, no Aunty please no,' and you feel foolish saying it because she barely looks older than you, even with her two drugged children and missing husband.

'Islam Hasan Ali!' she says. 'His name is Islam Hasan Ali! Please find him, please bring him home, please …'

She is crying to herself, no longer looking at you. You leave quietly. The image of the weeping woman on the floor, her head resting on the lax, lolling baby, his head fallen back at a non-human angle follows you.

Islam Hasan Ali. Salim Mohammedbhai. Nusrat Mohammedbhai.

Outside you blink in the sunshine but the smell of smoke is immediate and acrid. You begin to run.

Nusrat. You have to find Nusrat.

You can't find the school and you run through the streets again forever. Everything is spinning around you, the sun beating down hard on your head, the headache back and the pounding of your heart so loud between your eyes that you could barely see. Things flash by: a turned over vegetable cart with tomatoes split under sharp beaks of crows, a Hanuman temple with a headless Hanuman and a priest lying next to it, a mound of garbage, a dropped bag of bread, pamphlets in Marathi with pictures of swords and a smiling blue god sitting on a rock, a dog (Was it the dog from the store?) sitting solemnly on top of an empty cart, watching you run by for the second time as you try frantically to find a way to the school.

You run into the green and cream wall of the school. You climb over the gate and fall on the other side, hurting something in your left leg badly. You purse your lips and ignore it. You have a bad feeling you're running out of time.

Nusrat. You have to find Nusrat.

You run through the school and the red floors make you think of my house with its red-floor balcony and even as you're running, across the playground, through the corridor, with classrooms on the sides, you think about me and you wonder why I haven't written, if I'm alright. Because Nusrat was right, Tania Ghosh, you have a kind heart. A stupid, kind heart.

The shouting hits you like a wall of sound. You run out into the front courtyard of the school and you can see through the tall black posts of the front gate of the school that there are two big mobs facing each other, both with flags and swords and machetes and bricks and broken bottles still dripping with orange soda. One mob has men, women and children. The other mob has men.

You run to the gate. You grab the posts and look for Nusrat.

When you see her, your heart leaps in relief. She's right in the middle of the crowd, holding an older woman who must be her mother. Her mother is crying but Nusrat is dry-eyed and solemn, holding her mother tightly as if to prevent her from falling to the ground. She is jostled continually by the crowd and she ducks and flows with the crowd stoically. For a moment you just look at her, thinking how beautiful she is and how you can't wait to hold her hand and drag her away to safety. Your heart begins to slow down. It looks like a big shouting match but no one has hurt anyone. Maybe they will all go away. They won't hurt each other in front of a school.

It all happens quickly. One minute the men are just screaming at each other, a mix of slogans and abuse and indecipherable noise. The next minute, there are stones flying through the air and people falling to the ground. The women start screaming. The children start crying. You just keep your eye on Nusrat. She is being pushed and shoved. She puts her arm around her mother. She is trying to drag her to the side.

Suddenly a man breaks out from the mob with Nusrat in it. He runs across the empty space between the two crowds and enters the other mob. He has a large iron rod with him. He starts to hit men around him, waving his rod around. Blood blooms. The men in the other crowd close around the man and you can see the bodies pump up and down as they beat the man.

Suddenly police vans appear on the edges and scores of policemen pour out of them with revolvers in their hands. They jump into the crowds and disappear in the dust.

And then Nusrat runs after the man and disappears where the men are beating him.

You scream her name over and over again. NUSRAT! NUSRAT! NUSRAT!

But you can't see her anymore. She has disappeared. You begin to climb the gate to get to her.

And then the gunshots.

Once, twice, thrice.

Many times together. Many gun shots.

Everyone is screaming now and everyone is running in the

same direction—away from the square of confrontation, into lanes, into streets, into shops, into the dust growing opaque.

The dust is immense and through it you scream. NUSRAT! NUSRAT!

Your voice disappears into the mayhem and then quickly, as if it is a movie script, the square is silent and a moment ago where people had stood screaming at others, moments ago where there had been so many people beating Nusrat's father, moments ago where people were pushing and shoving and screaming, there is nothing but silence, nothing but dust.

You stop shouting and stand still, peering through the dust, hoping to see which direction Nusrat had run in. You are tired of running after her. You want to find her and you want to go home. You are beginning to feel angry.

NUSRAT! Let's go home now! NUSRAT! It's Tania!

NUSRAT, you scream through a now total silence, your voice ringing out into all corners. NUSRAT!

When the dust clears you see Nusrat. She is lying on the ground, on her side, looking straight at you.

For a moment you smile. She has seen you! Nusrat!

And then something is very wrong because how can her head be at that angle and who is that woman coming running towards her also calling her name and why isn't Nusrat getting up?

Nusrat! Nusrat! Nusrat!

The woman throws herself on Nusrat and you shout at her to not do that because who knows, maybe Nusrat broke a bone and you have to be really careful about not moving broken bones and why isn't the woman listening?

Nusrat! Nusrat!

Why isn't Nusrat getting up? Why isn't she smiling at her mother who is crying stupidly in a way that infuriates you?

Nusrat! Get up! We have to go home, Nusrat!

Nusrat! My parents are on their way. They are coming to get us! Come on Nusrat!

Nusrat! NUSRAT!

Three men come from nowhere with a stretcher that is half torn. One of them pulls Nusrat's mother away and you see that Nusrat's back is red, bright red, a red you have seen many times today. The men lift Nusrat and put her on the stretcher. Her head lolls forward and one of the men closes her eyes.

Nusrat! Nusrat stop acting! Nusrat! Come on get up! I'll take you to a better hospital! Nusrat it's not funny!

One of the men turns to look at you. Go away, he says. This is not for you. Go away.

NUSRAT! Nusrat!

You stand there watching them take away Nusrat.

You can't stop screaming her name even as the stretcher turns a corner and you can't see her anymore. You can't stop screaming her name even when your parents find you and it takes both of them to prise your hands off the school gate and you can't stop screaming her name all the way home in the car and you can't stop screaming her name when you're in your room and you see the mattress where she had slept last night and you can't stop screaming as you take the picture of her and you by the sea that you had taken the last time you both had gone there to throw popcorn at kissing couples and while you're screaming, while you're holding the picture to your heart as if it can mend what has happened inside, someone slides an injection in your arm and everything is finally, blessedly silent.

~

It takes you a week to find my letter. It takes that long because you are heavily sedated. You lose ten kilos and are admitted to the hospital. Every time you open your eyes you scream her name and you pull all the tubes out, hurting yourself and etching large blue and green bruises all over your body.

You can't bear to see anyone. Not your parents not Neenee not anyone.

On the eighth day you decide you want to go home so you allow the IV to pump into your body and you allow your mother to feed you and you allow them to put clothes on your body and take you home.

When you find the letter, you pick up the phone and call me. You tell me that I've killed Nusrat. You describe to me everything that happened. You tell me thirty-seven times that if it hadn't been for the letter, Nusrat would not have left the house. You read out the note she left you. The one in which she said, I will always love you more than anyone else in the world because you are my best friend. You tell me that she always has been your best friend. That she always will be your best friend. You tell me I am dead to you.

Your voice is clear and does not break. You do not let me speak. You hang up the phone and don't pick up when I call you back. I called you back seventeen times. From my house, from Ali's house, from a public telephone, from my school. You never pick up the phone. By the time I come out of the hospital for mad people, you have changed your number. You sent me all my letters, cut up in pieces.

It takes you three months to go see Nusrat's parents. You're stunned by how much it hurts to go to that old building, to see the corridor lit by a tube light, to see the drugged baby crawling carefully outside his house. His mother averts her eyes from you and pretends she does not recognise you.

It hurts even more to see her parents. Her eyes, older and full of tears. Her chin, so sharp like an old beloved question mark. Her hands, sure and finely veined. Her house is full of her certificates all of which have been framed and jostle for space. You finger the pictures of her, from when she was a baby at a studio with thick black kajal in her eyes, her fearless smile and bright green dress she would have made fun of when she was older. You try to suppress the feeling that if you just concentrate hard enough, your fingers will touch her and she will touch you back.

Her parents give you her tahveez that she had worn since she was a baby. They tell you that you were her best friend and that she loved you and that you made her happy. You want to break down and cry, on the older, rounder Nusrat shoulder and be comforted. You want to tell them what had happened and you want them to tell you that she knew you loved her. That she knew she was your best friend. But you never ask. Instead you put the tahveez around your neck and promise the old couple that you will not forget them, that you will visit them.

It takes you a year before you can go down to the sea again. On her birthday (she would have been eighteen and you had bought little gold earrings, the same pair for her and for you) you go down to the sea, the tahveez hot against the hollow of your throat.

At the sea, everything is the same. The same couples, the same children, the same dogs, the same smell of shit. It has taken you a long time to stop looking for her over your shoulder, feeling her hand on your hair, smelling her breath on your face, opening up her notebook to see what she has written. But here by the sea it comes back, the desire to have her next to you and it almost kills you, the intensity of knowing that she will never be there when you turn around.

The waves are still the same and you sit down on the rock and finally the tears that haven't come all year, come slowly and then with gathering force until your face is a hot river and you wish more than anything to become that river entirely and disappear into the sea. You realise that it will never stop hurting. You realise that every birthday, hers and yours, you will welcome the sadness because it will be the only way you have left of having her again, just for a little while. You realise that you've already forgotten little things, little gestures, little expressions and you wish for the thousandth time that you had taken the large, unwieldy home video camera to her and captured everything about her so that you would not have to live your life feeling yourself forget little by little.

When the tears finally stop, you take out a notebook that you found by going back to Nusrat's neighbourhood and going to the store that she used to go to. It's just like the one Nusrat always had.

*Dear Nusrat,*

*Happy birthday! You're eighteen today which is like totally an adult. I've been an adult for three months now which is awesome but it's really more of a feeling than anything else because it's not like anything is that different. I mean I can't even vote because my voter ID card has the picture of a GUY on it and he's not even cute. It's totally upsetting.*

*We sang Happy Birthday to you at our Peace Committee meeting today and your mom cried. The stupid school is again making noises about throwing us out because they are like worried that there will be more riots because you know the Shiv Sena is up to its tricks again.*

*But whatever, don't worry Nusrat. Because the riots won't happen again. We're doing this Peace Committee stuff in every sensitive neighbourhood which is what the police call any neighbourhood with a lot of Muslims in it. People play cricket and watch movies. I don't think the slum people even know what it's for—for them it's probably just like free cricket and movies and samosas and tea. But whatever, if it works who cares.*

*On your birthday there was a special match that your dad organised. I'm still a bit scared of him but he like ADORES me. He is so happy when I go to visit them. Anyway, today's match was* with the police and everyone was laughing at how funny the fat ones looked running between the wickets but I didn't laugh because I was so busy trying not to FAINT from the body odour.

So remember how I like do a brave Nusrat thing every month? Last month I did my classical dance recital. You know. You were there. I know you were there. Didn't I look sexy? If only my mom had let me make my blouse a little lower. She hates me obviously.

My brave Nusrat thing for this month is to go down to our spot by the sea. I'm sitting here now. You can like probably see me. I hope so because I'm wearing that shirt you really like, the purple one with polka dots that made you laugh.

There's a new guy in college who is pretty hot. All the losers from the suburbs call him the Western Looking Guy. Can you imagine? So ridiculous. But he totally checked me out today. I mean he better have. I was wearing my new jeans that make my butt look so good.

Anyway, HAPPY BIRTHDAY! I hope you're having super fun wherever you are and just for you, I just stopped writing and smiled at the sky. Did you see? I'm wearing the earrings I got for you and me. I gave yours to your mom to keep.

I'll never know if you knew, Nusrat. I keep going over and over that day in my mind but I don't know if you saw me. I wish I had told you that you are my best friend. I wish I had told you. I wish I had told you how much I liked it when you put your hand on my head and stroked my hair. I wish I had told you that when you put your arms around me that day when my mom was beating me, I felt so happy I thought my heart would burst. I wish I had told you that I love you more than anyone, even more than my mom and even more than my dad.

Anyway, I'm going to keep writing to you, you know. It's kind of like having you here. I'm going to use a pencil like you did. It's nice here right now, sitting where we used to sit. It's like you are here. And I can put my head on your shoulder and you will put your arm around me. Your hands are so soft and your arms are so strong.

*Nusrat, my Nusrat.*

*The sun is going down and I can't really see enough to keep writing so I guess I'll end here. I will always love you. Always have. Always will.*

*Yours,*
*Tania*

*PS—What do you think? It doesn't matter. I will still write to you. This is only a first letter.*

# Acknowledgements

Like every writer, I owe much to those who have supported this stubborn dreaming. To every writer I've read (especially the women writers), my grandfathers, my parents and my sister: thank you.

Thank you Himanjali Sankar, perspicacious editor and friend. Faiza Khan, Anurima Roy and everyone else at Bloomsbury India, thank you for your cheerful, canny support. I would never have inched beyond the idea without my wonderful friends who kept me going through innumerable bad starts and drafts. Strangers across the world have become mentors and friends in the writing of this book – thank you. Thank you Juthika Nagpal for being a sister to the girls, Nadia Majeed and Janice Huang for your needle-eyed reads amidst squalling babies and Chitra Ganguli, most exacting reader, whose memory of those days in 1992 kept it real. Thank you Shankar Ganguli for lighting the flame long ago and tending to it always. Every dreamer should have a champion like you.

Thank you Bombay and Karachi for being the beautiful, ugly, horror-ridden, life-giving cities that you are, stubbornly holding on to the banks of the grey Arabian, promising everything, giving everything and taking everything. No riot will destroy you and no one idea will overpower you. Here's to you and here's to the children who grow up in you.